Sunshine & Secrets

Sunshine & Secrets

DAISY JAMES

CANELO

First published in the United Kingdom in 2018 by Canelo

This edition published in the United Kingdom in 2019 by

Canelo Digital Publishing Limited
57 Shepherds Lane
Beaconsfield, Bucks HP9 2DU
United Kingdom

A CIP catalogue record for this book is available from the British Library.

Print ISBN 978 1 78863 413 7
Ebook ISBN 978 1 78863 016 0

Look for more great books at www.canelo.co

Printed and bound in Great Britain by Clays Ltd, Elcograf S.p.A.

To my wonderful family for their love, support and continuing willingness to taste-test all my recipes.

Chapter One

'Have you checked in yet, Millie?'

'No, but don't panic, Jen. I told you that I'd make an extra special effort to arrive in plenty of time, didn't I? I'm just grabbing a latte and a copy of *Hello!* before joining the queue – which, I have to tell you, is huge. Nice must be the place to be this month!'

Millie had no intention of admitting to her super-organized sister that the only reason she had arrived at Gatwick with time to spare was because Poppy had insisted on collecting her from her studio flat above Café Étienne that morning at a ridiculously early hour. Her friend and colleague had then driven them at stomach-wrenching speed to the airport and had marched her, still stuffing her passport into her hand luggage, to the check-in desk. Poppy had even offered to hang around until she made it through security just to make absolutely sure she didn't meet with some diversion and miss her flight – not an unknown, or indeed infrequent, occurrence.

'Great. I was hoping that you'd stuck to your usual schedule of taking every deadline down to the wire!'

Millie detected a note of excitement rather than impatience in Jen's voice. 'Why? What's happened?'

'Well, before you freak, just hear me out.'

'Jen, what's going on?' A coil of panic began to wind its way around her chest, just as it always did whenever arrangements got changed. Millie knew her reaction was something she would have to live with for the foreseeable future. It was just another item on the lengthy list of newly developed fears she had Luke to thank for.

'I know you're super-excited about spending your break from the café with Mum in Lourmarin, but the most fabulous opportunity has come up. If I wasn't booked to do a presentation at the Cornish Living show next weekend, I'd grab the chance myself.'

'Jen, please, you're killing me here.'

'Sorry. Okay, do you remember Claudia Croft? The celebrity cookery book writer who also runs culinary workshops and classes at her country manor in the Cotswolds? I helped her to deliver a couple of her Christmas tutorials last year? It was the most fabulous fun I've had for years!'

Millie allowed herself to relax a little. If her sister was talking about cooking, a passion they both shared, there was no cause for anxiety. She scanned the check-in queue and decided it was time to join the line for her flight to the South of France.

'Course I remember her. I also remember how envious I was when you got that gig!'

'Well, now I can make up for it. I've just spoken to Claudia. Sadly, she's broken her leg in a horse-riding accident. She's in hospital waiting for an operation. She was supposed to fly out to St Lucia today to supervise the finishing touches to her brand-new project – the Paradise Cookery School. She needs someone who knows what they're doing to go in her place, so, after I reluctantly told her I had to turn her offer down, I suggested you. It's perfect, Millie. You're more than qualified and a trip to St Lucia is just the opportunity you need to move on and start getting over what happened with Luke.'

'Jen, you know I'm…'

'So, as you can imagine, Claudia leapt at the chance to have a Cordon Bleu-trained chef to oversee the renovations. The school is being run at Claudia's villa in the hills overlooking the bay at

Soufrière in the south of St Lucia. Apparently, the builders have almost finished bringing the kitchen up to the professional standard needed to host a luxury cookery school so there won't be much for you to do except soak up the sunshine and explore the local cuisine. It'll be fantastic!'

'But Jen…'

'It's all organized. There's a ticket waiting for you at the British Airways desk – business class no less! Oh, Millie, I just know you're going to have the most amazing time out there. This is more like the sort of thing you should be doing instead of slaving away at that dingy little café in Hammersmith.'

'It's not a café, it's a French patisserie…'

'Mum thinks, and I happen to agree with her, that you just took the first job you were offered to get away from Oxford and everything that happened there. But it's been six months now, darling. I know how painful it was, but it's time to drag yourself out of the doldrums and start living again. Who knows, you might even have a holiday fling while you're there!'

'There is no way I'm going to have a holiday fling!'

'But it's a yes to going to St Lucia, though?'

The magazine Millie had been clutching under her arm, whilst juggling her mobile from ear to ear to improve the signal, clattered onto the marble floor and she sloshed a generous splash of coffee down her white Capri pants. Before she could bend to retrieve it, a tall, designer-clad guy with mirrored sunglasses crouched down and scooped it up, gifting her with a flash of his brilliant white teeth.

'Erm, thanks.'

The George Clooney lookalike bowed his head in acknowledgement before sauntering towards the news stand, glancing back over his shoulder in Millie's direction as he selected a copy of the *Daily Telegraph*. Heat rose to her cheeks and she averted her eyes.

'Millie? Millie, are you still there? Are you listening to me?'

'Sorry. Just a little coffee mishap. I'm still here. Mum's going to be disappointed. I think she had lots of things planned for me.'

'I called Mum before I called you. She's fine about it. And don't tell me you were looking forward to attending her G&T soirées with the local Salsa club. Did she tell you her friend Solange has had her navel pierced? She's seventy! I warned Mum that I'd disown her if she followed suit.'

Jen released an impatient sigh at the antics of their youthful, energetic mother – a response Millie had grown familiar with over the years since their father had passed away and Monique had returned to her home town of Lourmarin to reinvent herself as a social butterfly.

'So, is it a yes?'

Millie blew her fringe, the colour of summer wheat, away from her eyelashes. She could almost hear the steamroller's engine revving up behind her, but she allowed herself a wry smile. She was pleased to see that her sister had confidence in her organizational skills – which was more than the evidence on offer warranted – and a couple of weeks in the sunshine certainly appealed to her.

'Okay, it's a yes. What exactly does Claudia want me to do?'

'The villa is part of an old cocoa plantation which Claudia and her husband Tim renovated a few years ago to use as a holiday retreat from the frazzled lifestyle they lead in London. There's an estate manager who lives on site to look after the grounds and the buildings, but that's a full-time job in itself and Claudia feels he's too busy to make absolutely sure the kitchen upgrade will be finished to an ultra-high spec. The first workshop is scheduled for two weeks' time. It's a pre-wedding bonding bash, organized and paid for by the bride's mother for her daughter's bridesmaids and girl-friends to have fun and to relax before the main event. They're staying at a five-star hotel nearby, where the wedding ceremony will take place in a pavilion in the grounds – so romantic!'

'And Claudia is sure she'll be well enough to fly out to take the classes?'

'Absolutely!'

'Good, because I don't know the first thing about running a cookery school.'

'Claudia told me that the week-long course is called Chocolate & Confetti and will be focusing on all things chocolate-related. Apparently, the plantation used to grow cocoa beans commercially until fairly recently when the business became unviable and the estate was put up for sale. Claudia is planning to produce cocoa from the estate for use in the cookery schools, at some point in the future. And anyway, Millie darling, even if she isn't fully recovered, you could handle the classes with your eyes closed. It's not the baked *Faisan en Croûte* with *foie gras* or the *Lapin à la Cocotte* you were used to producing before… well, before your change in career direction, is it?'

'Stop the flattery, Jen. I'm your sister, I can see right through you.'

Jen laughed, the relief evident in her voice. 'Thanks for doing this, Millie. I owe you one. And will you humour me by keeping an open mind on the holiday romance?'

Millie didn't want Jen to venture into the pain-strewn territory of romance. She swallowed down hard on her rising emotions, swivelled on her stiletto sandals and dragged her wheelie suitcase towards the British Airways desk, thanking her guardian angel that she had at least packed the right clothes for a trip to the Caribbean. Her mum had warned her that Provence was experiencing one of the warmest Septembers on record.

'Look, Jen...'

'It's been six months now, Millie. You've got to break free from the mist of misery you've taken refuge in. So, it hurts – but it's just a blip in life's grenade-dotted path. Happiness could be just around the corner if you take the chance to explore the landscape and get some perspective. Failing that, you could just opt for some *lurve* in the sun!'

'I am exploring...' Millie murmured. But in truth she knew her life was like the reverse side of one of her mother's embroidery projects; knotted and disorganized, waiting for the creator to switch the fabric round to display the beauty of the front.

'What? As a pastry chef in a tiny café in a drab side street in London?'

'It's a patisserie…' Millie repeated but she knew Jen wasn't listening.

'That's not exploring, that's punishment after everything you've achieved in the culinary arena. Hey, Lily, stop that! Look, I have to go before the girls start bickering. I'll email you all the info and the photos – the villa is truly stunning. And Claudia will be so grateful. Have you got your scrap box with you?'

'I've always got my scrap box with me.'

Millie patted her straw shoulder bag and was comforted by the reassuring presence of the lever-arch box file that never left her sight. It was crammed to bursting with recipes, snippets of foodie articles, glossy photographs of unusual dishes, information on a newly discovered spice and its potential uses. There was no elaborate filing system for Amelia Harper – she'd meant to get one started, but who had the time?

'Good. Now, go grab your ticket and enjoy the flight. Lucky you! It's free Prosecco, you know. I love you, Millie.'

'Love you too, Jen.'

I think, she thought.

Chapter Two

'Why are we stopping?'

'I'm sorry, madam, but I'll have to drop you off here. There's no way my old taxi will make it up the hill to the house in this rain.'

'But you can't leave me here! We're in the middle of a hurricane!'

The elderly taxi driver chuckled at Millie's exaggeration.

'This is no hurricane, my dear. It's merely the St Lucian daily deluge. Look.' He tapped the face of his incongruously large diver's watch and treated her to a display of his tobacco-stained teeth. 'It's three o'clock. It'll be over in twenty minutes and I promised to collect Ella from Soufrière and bring her back to the villa to meet you. So go on, hop out into what we Caribbean natives call the liquid sunshine!'

Millie stared out of the windscreen. It was like being in a car wash. She had never experienced anything like it, even during her visits to see Luke's parents in Snowdonia. Torrential rain hammered down from a canopy of leaden clouds onto the steep strip of tarmac that led up to Claudia Croft's plantation house. Multiple rivulets of water chased down the slope and the palm trees lining the access road tilted almost horizontally to the storm's demands. She cursed her misplaced optimism that her two-week break in St Lucia would be filled with long, sun-soaked days stretched out in a hammock by the pool, cocktail in hand, a gentle tropical breeze rippling through the air.

She cast a last glance at the taxi driver, who had introduced himself as Clavie, in the rear-view mirror, gathered her straw shoulder bag and resigned herself to a soaking. As she cracked opened the taxi door, a volley of raindrops attacked her with such vengeance that within seconds she was drenched. She had a premonition that whilst this was the first time she had experienced the phenomenon of 'liquid sunshine', it would not be the last.

Her hair was plastered to her cheeks and her strappy scarlet T-shirt clung to the contours of her body. She twisted her lips at the amusement scrawled across Clavie's wrinkled face and slammed the door with as much force as she could muster after nine hours of long-haul travel. She noticed that he made no attempt to exit his warm, comfortable, *dry* seat to extricate her luggage from the boot. So much for chivalry, thought Millie as she hooked her stiffened fingers around the handle of her overstuffed suitcase and heaved it over the lip of the boot before dropping it with a thud onto her toe.

'Ouch!'

But Clavie simply gave her a brief wave and sped away, the mellifluous tones of a calypso rhythm spilling from his ancient vehicle, which was more rust than bucket.

She was now soaked to her underwear and had to fight the urge to sit down amongst the tropical vegetation at the edge of the road and indulge in a fit of sobbing. Not only had she endured a flight delay, she had also been forced to wait over an hour for her luggage to arrive on the tiny carousel at Hewanorra airport. She could have collected it from the hold quicker herself. Then, the incredibly turbulent ride from the airport to Soufrière in the taxi had just about finished her off. Yes, the scenery had been spectacular, but she felt as though her bones had been shaken to dust.

Why had she agreed to come? Was she even *capable* of supervising the installation of a professional-standard kitchen and making sure everything was ready for the first of the Paradise

Cookery School tutorials? She squashed her demons of self-doubt back into their box for later dissection. There was no way she was going to open the cupboard door on all her yesterdays when the only thing she wanted to do was strip off her wet clothes and sleep.

Millie had received the promised email from Jen and had studied the attachments during the flight. It turned out her sister hadn't told her the full story – nothing new there. Not only did she have to oversee the renovations but she was also expected to triple-test and finalize the course recipes and menu cards. It was going to be a challenge – it would be years before she could aspire to match the brilliance of Claudia Croft, if ever. She was relieved that Claudia had arranged for her friend and local Caribbean cook, Ella Johnson, to be an integral part of the testing committee. Despite the course attendees' desire to indulge in a fun-filled, pre-wedding celebration, Millie knew that the price the bride's mother had paid for the classes meant they would be a discerning and demanding audience – foodies with an interest in furthering their skills and repertoire to include a cocoa-flavoured twist.

So, a siesta was obviously out of the question. Ella would be arriving shortly to meet her and Millie wanted to reassure her that she was up to the job. She straightened her shoulders, grabbed the handle of her wheelie suitcase and drew in a lungful of breath. The sweet fragrance of jasmine, mingled with wet soil, tickled her nostrils as she dragged her luggage and her exhausted body up the incline towards the house. She slung her bag higher up her shoulder so she could protect her trusty scrap box of recipes with her arm, and tossed her bedraggled mermaid hair over her shoulder, wishing she had thought to tie it back. Her jerky movement dislodged an apple from the top of her bag and it rolled away down the hill, picking up speed until it rounded the corner and disappeared from view.

The daily deluge continued its onslaught. The celestial director of meteorology had clearly decided to ratchet up the special effects for her arrival on stage. Unexpectedly, Millie felt tears gather along her lashes. Not only was she soaked to the skin, with a throbbing toe and burning lungs from the unfamiliar exertion of tackling the hill, now a juggernaut of tiredness had rammed into her bones.

However, her excursion into self-pity didn't last long. As she emerged from a dense grove of banana trees, the welcome sight of the old planta-tion house erased her lethargy in an instant. Built in the French colonial style, with a white-painted veranda and pale blue jalousie shutters, the villa nestled comfortably against the tropical foliage of the rainforest. The building was impressive but she was too exhausted to fully appreciate its architectural splendour.

She ditched her luggage next to a stack of scarred wooden crates, stuffed to bursting with weird-looking purple-brown pods, loitering on the doorstep like sentries, and trotted around the wooden veranda to the front of the house. What she saw whipped the breath from her lungs.

A set of smooth white marble steps descended towards the most stunning expanse of aquamarine she had ever seen. The infinity pool's decking had been embellished with six navy-and-white striped sunloungers and was bordered by a necklace of lush banana trees, their leaves sporting a glossy sheen from the recent downpour. But she barely noticed this arboreal glory compared to the majesty of the panorama in front of her widened eyes. She felt her jaw drop.

To her left, the twin peaks of Gros Piton and Petit Piton reared up from the azure of the Caribbean Sea like two ancient pyramids swathed in a mantle of undulating emerald velvet. At their foot nestled the old French capital of St Lucia,

Soufrière, its church spire and telegraph poles jutting from a patchwork of red-roofed homes stitched together by palm trees.

Despite the dribbles of perspiration mingled with raindrops that were scuttling down the back of her neck, Millie couldn't drag her eyes away from the display of nature's perfection. This was her idea of paradise and Claudia had certainly picked the most apt name for her new venture – with a view like this the Paradise Cookery School couldn't fail to be a success. She felt the tension of the last few hours melt from her temples and join the streams of sweat on their journey southwards.

'Ahh,' she breathed, momentarily unable to conjure up words sufficient to do justice to the landscape. Even in the pouring rain it was so perfect that it seemed almost unreal; a painting or a movie set created for a Hollywood producer who had demanded a glorious depiction of the Garden of Eden in all its technicoloured splendour.

Millie fished around in her shoulder bag for her phone to check the instructions for locating the key. Much as she would have loved to stay in the villa, she was more than happy to have been allocated a studio in the modern addition to the property – a pristine garage complex at the other side of a courtyard with housing for three vehicles and a small apartment above boasting floor-to-ceiling windows and a cute wrought-iron balcony. The front door and the shutters had been painted blue in keeping with the theme of the main house and a smile of satisfaction curled at the corners of her lips. She might have arrived in the middle of a monsoon, but this was a little slice of heaven.

She located the key under a large ceramic pot containing a tumble of crimson geraniums and dragged her luggage up the stairs. Abandoning her suitcase in the hallway, she cast her eyes around her temporary home. Compared to her cramped cupboard under the eaves of Café Étienne where she worked, this apartment was a palace. She adored the whitewashed, vaulted ceiling with a lazy fan wafting the air and the voile curtains around the bed. The open-plan living area boasted two over-stuffed white sofas resting on bleached wooden floorboards, and whilst the kitchen wasn't huge it was still larger than her own. She peeled off her travelling clothes and gathered her hair into the pretty hair tie Poppy had given her as a going-away present.

Poppy! What would her friend say when she told her that instead of spending two weeks with her dance-obsessed mother in Provence, she had diverted her route to the Caribbean and was staying for a fortnight in the lap of luxury. A sharp spasm of loneliness shot through her chest. How fabulous it would have been to share her good fortune with Poppy, but then, wasn't she supposed to be in St Lucia to work? She made a promise to herself that when she got back to London, she would make a concerted effort to socialize more, and not just to stop Poppy and Jen from lecturing her.

She strolled to the French doors and looked out to the balcony. Once again, the spectacular view stole her attention until she wrenched her thoughts back to the challenge ahead. Claudia was relying on her to get this right. With over twenty cookery books published, a popular vlog and a YouTube channel with thousands of subscribers, Claudia Croft was well respected in the baking-enthusiast community in the UK and beyond. Plus, she had a proven track record in delivering bespoke culinary courses, having perfected her skills at the Claudia Croft Cotswolds Cookery School over the last ten years. Claudia's eagerly anticipated debut into gastronomic education in the Caribbean had to go without a hitch and Millie knew there could be no allowances made for her tendency to flirt with calamity. A frisson of trepidation shot down her spine and fizzled out to her fingertips.

She scrolled through her phone until she reached Claudia's email setting out the details of the renovations:

> The precise layout of the kitchen area has been architecturally designed to enhance the available space as well as take full advantage of the view whilst the Paradise Cookery School's guests prepare their culinary masterpieces. It is imperative that every detail, however insignificant, be adhered to by the builders. It's your job, Millie, to ensure they do this. It's as simple as that. As an accomplished chef yourself, I know you're going to love what I've chosen. I've sourced the marble countertops from Italy and the cabinets are handmade by a manufacturer in Germany. The crate containing the cabinetry and the kitchen appliances should have already arrived at Soufrière. The delivery company have assured me that the incline is not an issue.

Millie did not share their optimism. If her taxi driver's reticence was anything to go by, she hoped the kitchen delivery men would at least avoid the 'daily deluge' time slot.

> The carpenters, electrician and plumber will all begin work first thing on Monday morning. There's a clause in the contract that says the work must be finalized to my specification by the following Friday, but I'm sure we won't need to refer to this. The men come highly recommended and I have every faith in them finishing in time for the wedding party to start their Chocolate & Confetti tutorials on the Monday morning.

A sharp nip of anxiety pierced Millie's chest. Two weeks to fit any kitchen was pushing it, never mind one as high-spec as Claudia wanted.

> Now for the most important part. All the recipes that are being featured on the course have been drafted, but they still need to be triple-tested on site before I authorize their inclusion. That's where you come in, Millie. I know the kitchen in the studio is tiny, but it should be okay for what you

need to do and I've arranged for the cupboards to be stocked with everything you need. I have also engaged the services of Ella Johnson, a highly respected St Lucian chef, to assist you as I want every recipe to be as authentic as possible. Ella has many years of experience cooking with the spices produced on the island and has access to recipes that have been passed down through generations of St Lucian cooks. I just know you two will get on like a house on fire.

Millie's stomach lurched to her toes and back. Claudia made it sound like they were rehearsing for roles in a theatrical show – certainly the final performance would be in front of an audience, so maybe that was exactly what it *was* like. Still, there was a lot to achieve in just two weeks. With difficulty, she tore her eyes away from the view and trotted down the stairs to see if the taxi driver had managed to negotiate the hill and deliver Ella to the villa. She couldn't wait to meet her.

The monsoon was still baring its teeth, refusing to slacken its ferocity, and within seconds she was drenched to the skin again. She jogged across the courtyard and was about to take the path towards the pool terrace when, despite the downpour, she stopped in her tracks.

Was that a dog barking?

She squinted into the foliage to her right and thought her eyes must be playing tricks on her. What looked like a dark silhouette loitered on the periphery of the tangled trees. As the shadow grew closer, it took on the shape of a grizzly bear. Did they have bears in St Lucia? Her heart thudded – a bass drumbeat to accompany the symphony of pounding rain and her sporadic breathing.

At the same time as the figure emerged from its forest camouflage, a loud *woof* rang through the air and a cannonball of fur launched itself at her. For the briefest of moments, she had a vision that she was about to be mauled to death, one limb at a time, by a rabid Caribbean beast and the howl of objection that erupted from her lips could have matched the intensity of any horror-movie wolf. She continued to scream, her lungs ablaze with the fire of fear, her throat hoarse and dry. Her mind blurred then stalled, her internal mutterings making no sense. Her legs seemed to have frozen on the spot, their control disconnected from her brain and refusing to respond to her need to engage the 'flight' option – she was no good at the 'fight' alternative.

An upswing of serrated emotion rolled through her veins. Why did this always have to happen to her?

Millie flung her arms over her head to protect her face and spun round. The heel of her sandal caught in a crack between the paving stones and she was jettisoned, bottom first, into a very inconveniently placed puddle.

'Argh!'

She cowered, expecting the sharp stab of an incisor to impale her skin any second. Instead, she felt a warm, wet tongue licking the raindrops from her cheeks and depositing a generous splodge of drool on her chin and the back of her hand.

'Euww!'

A welcome wave of relief washed over her when she peeped through her fingers and saw the friendly face of a black-and-white Springer spaniel, followed immediately by an almost overwhelming surge of exhaustion. When she thought about it, her over-the-top reaction could be put down to the fact that she had been awake for over twenty-four hours and her body was screaming its objection to her lack of recent indulgence in restorative sleep.

'Don't worry, Binks won't hurt you unless I ask him to. Here, let me help you up.'

She accepted the man's outstretched hand and allowed him to pull her upright.

'Don't tell me you're one of those people who are scared of dogs? Or, judging by the expression of horror on your face at our arrival, maybe it's not just the canine fraternity that upsets you? Perhaps your phobia extends to the whole of the animal kingdom?'

Millie was temporarily struck mute at the prickly, suspicious words of her rescuer. With tufted mahogany hair, eyes the colour of liquid coal, a cute nose and a welcome added dash of the height gene – he was movie-star handsome. She couldn't quite place his accent. Unfortunately, irritation exuded from his pores and he was clearly expecting for her to say something.

'What?'

'Oh, I'm sorry. I guess I was just waiting for your effusive thanks for helping you out of that crater you threw yourself into, and then for you to explain why you are trespassing on private property.'

Millie opened and closed her mouth in amazement. The guy wasn't just prickly, he was downright rude. She was about to launch into a speech about civility when her teeth started to chatter and a bout of violent shivering overtook her. She wrapped her arms around her waist and her new adversary reluctantly removed his jacket and draped it over her shoulders. With a brief glance at the column of wooden crates stacked at the villa's front door, he guided her towards one of the cane chairs on the villa's covered veranda, his faithful attack dog at his heels.

'So? What are you doing here?'

'I'm Amelia Harper. Claudia Croft has engaged me to oversee the kitchen renovations for the first of her Paradise Cookery School courses in the Caribbean. She's had… She's unable to make it over to St Lucia until the end of next week.' Millie didn't want to disclose any information about Claudia's personal circumstances to the stranger who was now wearing a look of extreme scepticism on his face.

'How do I know you are who you say you are?' The man rolled his eyes in an exaggerated gesture. 'Mrs Croft usually vets all her staff and emails through their references before they arrive. I was expecting a Mrs Jennifer Bertrand and you look nothing like her.'

'Jennifer Bertrand is my sister. She couldn't make it and so I came instead.'

'So you just thought you would step seamlessly into your sister's shoes?'

'I beg your pardon! I *am* qualified, you know! Not that it's any of your business, but I have excellent credentials in the culinary field.'

Again, Millie could hear the defensive tone that had crept into her vocabulary since the debacle with Luke and she didn't like it – she really *had* to work on reacquainting herself with her former assertiveness. Her usually imperceptible French accent had also strengthened as her emotions churned, and the heat rising in her chest had nothing to do with the warmth of the weak rays of sunlight that were at last poking through the pewter canopy overhead, ratcheting up the temperature and causing wisps of steam to rise from the surrounding vegetation.

Who did this man think he was, cross-examining her on the reasons for her presence? Nevertheless, she experienced an overwhelming need to justify herself to him.

'Until six months ago, I was head chef at a Michelin-starred bistro in Oxford. I have more than enough expertise to oversee the installation of a commercial kitchen, even one of such high calibre as this one! Anyway, I don't have to reel off my qualifications to you. As I said,

Claudia approved my appointment as Jen's substitute personally.'

'Ahh, the arrogance of the French.'

'I happen to find your comment offensive,' Millie retorted, before adding unnecessarily 'Anyway, I'm *half* French.'

As soon as she had spoken, the mask of suspicion melted from the man's face and was replaced by amusement. Dimples appeared at the corners of his lips and laughter, with a soupçon of mischief, danced in his eyes as he took in her damp clothes from her unscheduled dip in the puddle and the confetti of fallen flower petals that had become lodged in her hair.

'So, now that we've ascertained your rudeness about my presence here was unwarranted, why don't we find out who *you* are and why *you* are here? Are you one of the gardeners?'

The man's smile widened as he patted Binks. 'No. I'm Zach Barker, Tim and Claudia's estate manager back in the UK. I'm here temporarily, responsible for the smooth running of the plantation and the upkeep of the grounds whilst my colleague is visiting his sick mother in Cheltenham.'

A sudden thought occurred to Millie. 'Do you live in the villa?'

'No way!' Zach laughed then smirked at the relief scrawled across Millie's face. 'Don't worry, Binks and I won't be getting in your way. We live in a very comfortable lodge on the other side of the plantation. Now, why don't I call Ella to see where she's got to while you get out of those damp clothes. You look like you just rolled off a pathologist's slab.'

'Charming,' she muttered.

Millie returned Zach's jacket to him before making her way to the studio, feeling his eyes scorching a hole into her back as she went. She prayed that she wouldn't trip or fall over her two left feet again. She didn't want to give him any additional fuel to enflame his character assessment of her.

She stripped to her underwear and selected a sunflower-yellow spaghetti-strapped T-shirt and a pair of white denim shorts before pushing her toes into sparkly flip-flops. As she grabbed a bottle of water from the fridge, an unexpected surge of homesickness ambushed her. The Croft plantation was a stunningly picturesque place to be but, if her first brush with the other member of Claudia's staff was anything to go by, she would much rather be paraded on the dance floor by her kaftan-bedecked mother.

Before she could stop herself, tears of loneliness trickled down her cheeks as she stared at the bucolic panorama from her balcony, still mesmerized by its hypnotic beauty. She wiped her eyes and gave herself a good talking-to. If she had been given this amazing opportunity six months ago she would have squeezed every last drop of enjoyment out of it. She resolved to do as Jen had suggested – to use the time and space to move on – and she should start by making an effort with Zach. She squared her shoulders and went back down the stairs to the courtyard.

'Okay. I've spoken to Ella and she should be here in fifteen minutes. Hey, have you been crying?'

'No. Of course not.'

Zach narrowed his eyes, but decided against delivering another one of his pithy comments on her blatant lie. He called Binks to heel and strode away down the driveway.

'Where are you going?' Millie called, disappointed that her resolution to get to know Zach better was a non-starter. She also didn't want to admit that his sudden and unexpected appearance from the tropical rainforest earlier had unnerved her. Who, or more to the point, *what* else could be lurking in there?

'Well, as a lowly "gardener" my responsibilities are many, Princess Sparkle-Toes.' Zach swept his gaze to her flip-flops and took in her multi-coloured pedicure, courtesy of Poppy during a pre-holiday girly session that involved glittery varnish and copious amounts of her favourite pink Prosecco. 'After you've met up with Ella you'll be able to spend the rest of the evening polishing your tiara and rustling up one of your Michelin-starred creations us mere mortals can't possibly be expected to appreciate. Oh, and don't forget to get your quota of beauty sleep required by all royal personalities. You're going to need it!'

Zach grinned, displaying a perfect set of teeth that any orthodontist worth his weight in toothpaste would be proud of. Millie slumped down into a cane chair on the veranda. She hoped she got on better with Ella Johnson because if Zach was going to be her only other company at the Paradise Cookery School she was in for a turbulent time.

Chapter Three

With a chorus of birdsong and croaking crickets to accompany her thoughts, Millie meandered along the pathway between the swimming pool and the edge of the plantation. In the post-deluge afternoon sunshine, she could completely understand why Claudia had fallen in love with the villa. Its position on the hillside overlooking the most famous of St Lucia's landmarks must be one of the best in the Caribbean.

Cocoa palms crammed the estate for as far as the eye could see. Strange wizened pods, the shape of small rugby balls, grew straight out of the gnarled trunks. She ran her fingertips over one of them, prodding the leathery, purple-brown exterior. She sniffed the skin, expecting it to smell of chocolate, but unsurprisingly it didn't. These were the husks she had seen piled in the wooden crates by the back door of the villa earlier. She assumed Zach had harvested them.

She regretted not having the chance to chat through the finer details for the school with Claudia. She hoped her vision would be, if not identical, then along similar lines to the celebrated cookery writer's own. Whilst the plans were already approved, it would be the finishing touches that made a project like the Paradise Cookery School stand out from the rest. A loop of nervousness began to coil around her chest when she thought of the responsibility of testing out the recipes for such a prestigious venture. What if she got it wrong?

Millie immediately chastised herself for her negativity. Only a few short months ago, she would never have entertained such an episode of self-doubt. It was amazing how a broken heart could deflate a person's confidence so much, even in their professional life! She inhaled a deep breath and vowed to concentrate on the advantages of her good fortune; the opportunity not only to learn new culinary techniques from Ella but also to experiment with a medley of fresh, exotic ingredients, all under the sparkling canopy of the Caribbean sky.

To say she was a sun-worshipper was an understatement. After all, she had spent the first seven years of her life and every summer holiday thereafter with her French grandparents running through the lavender-infused fields in the South of France until her limbs were as brown as milk chocolate. However, for some reason, she had chosen to overlook the fact that for such a lush tropical paradise to exist in St Lucia there inevitably had to be a regular delivery of rain in almost biblical proportions. Never mind. It couldn't rain all the time and she was looking forward to enjoying the golden beaches and mooching around the brightly painted shops in Soufrière with the strains of calypso music spilling out onto the pathways – not to mention sampling the local rum cocktails.

She would continue to work on healing her wounded heart whilst proving to Claudia that she had made a worthy choice by showing off her wide range of culinary skills to their best advantage. It was something she hadn't been able to do whilst working as one of a number of pastry chefs at the patisserie. The only talents she had exhibited to the patient French owner, Étienne, were her complete lack of organizational skills and her propensity to sprinkle ingredients and culinary implements like an escaped garden hose.

The intense screech of a struggling car engine, accompanied by a loud blast of reggae music, told her that Clavie had arrived with Ella Johnson. Her spirits lifted and she jogged back to the veranda and into the courtyard to welcome her, hopeful that this time she was about to meet a friendly companion with whom she had lots in common.

She watched the woman emerge from the back seat of the taxi and was relieved the driver had managed to navigate the incline this time. The Caribbean chef carried a few extra pounds around her midriff – enhanced by the brightly coloured fabric of her voluminous dress. A bold statement necklace rested at her chest and matching gold hoops hung from her lobes. She had rounded the ensemble off with a wide emerald-and-saffron bandana to keep her hair away from her smooth, crease-free forehead.

'Hello! You must be Millie!'

Ella rushed towards Millie and enveloped her in a fragrant hug, drawing her into her ample bosom as though enjoying a reunion with a long-lost daughter. Her lips glistened with a slick of deep burgundy lipstick, but her eyes had no need of shadow or mascara. The dark hazel of her irises drew the onlooker's attention to their kindness and wisdom. A faint whiff of lavender, mingled with a sweet caramel, tickled at Millie's nostrils.

'*Sooo* good to meet you. Claudia has told me all about you,' she cooed before turning to the taxi driver. 'Thanks, Clavie. See you Saturday?'

Ella's accent was a melodious sonata of French mingled with St Lucian Creole, which fell softly on the ear. Straight away Millie felt a strong connection with this woman who seemed to project an irresistible aura of comfort and competence. She wouldn't admit it out loud but Ella reminded her of her mother; the way Monique moved, her Gallic gestures, the cadence in her voice, the calm that exuded from every pore no matter what calamity her daughter had perpetrated, the partiality for wearing bright colours. She was certainly an inspired choice as a co-presenter of an upmarket Caribbean cookery school.

'Sure thing, man. Send my regards to that son of yours, okay?'

'Oh, I will!'

Ella linked her plump arm through Millie's and guided her to a pair of blue-and-white striped canvas chairs on the veranda of the villa where they could appreciate the view. Ella's afro curls bounced as she swivelled in her seat to fix Millie with her chestnut gaze, clearly weighing her up until her eyes came to rest on Millie's hair.

'I see you've had first-hand experience of the rain we get here!' There was that belly laugh again. 'Clavie told me he'd ditched you at the bottom of the driveway, the old goat!'

Millie reached up to run her fingers through her long straw-like fringe and down the sides to her shoulders. The usually sleek strands seemed to have doubled in volume as the humidity increased.

'Is there anything you can recommend that might tame my hair?'

'A little coconut oil may help – or you could just go with the flow. You'll have to tie it back when we start cooking anyway. Now, I have the keys to the villa so you'll be able to get an idea of what Claudia has planned, but I'm sure you've noticed the fact that very little progress has been made on the kitchen renovations. The builders were supposed to start their preparations last week but there was a delay in the delivery of the appliances due to some administrative mix-up. Why they couldn't have got on with something else I don't know, but it means the schedule is going to be tighter than initially thought.'

Ella paused and placed her hand over Millie's. 'If you'll allow me to give you a little friendly advice, Millie. Under no circumstances must you allow the men to take advantage of your good nature. Time is elastic to Fitz and whilst he's renowned island-wide for being the best in the business, he does have an equally infamous tendency to slope off for a lunchtime rum and a nap. As the final touches will be down to us, it is our time he will be stealing!'

Millie smiled, grateful that she had such a strong-willed ally in her corner. She wished Ella had been around to stand up for her when she had met Zach earlier, but she decided not to mention the fact that she had made his acquaintance, as she wasn't sure she would be able to keep her irritation at his treatment of her out of her voice. With any luck, she wouldn't have much to do with him over the next two weeks.

'Thanks, I'll bear that in mind.'

'Good. I can already see that we are on the same wavelength! Okay, shall we acquaint ourselves with the plans for the kitchen and then we can have a chat about the best part – the Paradise Cookery School recipes?'

'Yes, please.'

Ella drew back the bi-folding doors at the front of the villa to reveal a large empty space. Devoid of all its furniture and appliances, the room was huge. Rectangular in shape, one side had been constructed completely from glass windows to take advantage of the view and all the walls had been painted white – a perfect blank canvas and an ideal space for a boutique cookery school. A lone ceiling fan rotated languidly but Millie was relieved to see there was an industrial-sized air-conditioning unit on the back wall. A door to the right of the kitchen led to a corridor.

'You'll find bedrooms through there,' Ella said, pointing in the direction of Millie's gaze. 'Claudia is toying with the idea of offering accommodation to the gastronomes at some point in the future but not until the school is up and running and she can gauge the demand for her courses. Here are the plans.' Ella gestured to the back of the room where two large sheets of paper had been pinned to the wall. 'There'll be one large demonstration work-bench for Claudia and four smaller ones which can house two students each. It's a simple enough layout and should be easily completed within the two weeks, provided Fitz and his men turn up on time on Monday morning. I've checked and the lorry *is* booked for seven a.m.'

Millie studied the drawings and resolved to ensure that she was acquainted with every detail before Monday. She did not want to let Claudia down, but from the little experience she had of building work, everything always took longer than expected. The builders would have to work long days to get it finished on time.

She followed Ella back outside to the veranda and feasted her eyes on the pool, its surface reflecting the sky above like an aquamarine mirror. She took in the terracotta pots crammed to bursting with bright orange begonias as well as the sweeping palms offering essential shade to the avid sun-worshipper. She wondered whether she would have any spare time to take a dip in its cool waters.

'Claudia adores this house. She's spent a small fortune on restoring it to its former glory. But her true passion lies in the plantation itself. One day she hopes to grow cocoa commercially again and to offer guided tours of the plantation with sampling. It's the reason she set up the cookery school – to encourage visitors.'

'I can see why. The place is absolutely my idea of paradise.'

'Ah, but when she and Tim bought the estate, it was in a dreadfully dilapidated state and the cocoa crop had been left to rot on the trees. Harvesting the pods is such a labour-intensive activity that it was no longer worth the effort. But the trees are a variety called Trinitario, which produces the very best cocoa beans. Claudia engaged an expert in the cultivation of cocoa to check on the health of the trees and to advise her on their care. With his help, she has planted new saplings, grafted from their older cousins, and even started to harvest some of the pods – following the old methods of maturing, fermenting, drying, then finally roasting the beans in an outdoor oven built specially for the job.'

'So that's what's in those crates by the front door?' Millie couldn't wait to investigate the unfamiliar fruit further by performing a gastronomic autopsy.

'Yes. And that's why the first Paradise Cookery School courses will focus on all things cocoa-related.' Ella paused as she cast her eyes over the cocoa trees that congregated at the other side of the infinity pool. 'Did you know it's not just the cocoa *beans* we use? The white flesh from the pods can be used in rum-based cocktails. Andrew, the owner of the Purple Parrot in Soufrière, makes a mean daiquiri – Andy's Blast, he calls it. I'll ask Henri to take you to sample one of his liquid masterpieces. Mind you only indulge in the one, though. Andrew has a loose wrist when it comes to the spirits in his signature drinks!'

'Henri?'

'My son. He's a journalist during the day and a bit of a rum connoisseur when the sun dips over the horizon,' she laughed, a full-body rumble from deep within her chest which made Millie smile. Clearly Ella adored her son and was proud of his profession. 'I'm sure you'll have plenty in common.

He studied for his degree in Bordeaux. It was the only decent thing his father ever did for him.'

A cloud flitted over Ella's face – a faint tightening of her jawline, the colour of melted chocolate – but she swiftly erased it.

'Sorry. Anyway, as you know, Claudia wants every one of her recipes triple-tested before they're allowed to feature on the final menu. We'll be offering the students lunch though, so we'll need a couple of standby dessert recipes to complement the fish dishes.'

'What about a tarte au citron, but made with limes? There're loads in the grounds and it's one of my favourite recipes.'

'Sounds delicious. I'm really hoping this new venture of Claudia's takes off. This part of St Lucia needs all the enterprise it can get. It'll also be a chance to showcase our amazing culinary heritage to a wider audience. If the first course is a flop, or even if there are teething problems, you know what people are like. They'll tear it apart in a mean-spirited review and the Paradise Cookery School will be over before it's started.'

'Don't worry, Ella. Nothing will go wrong.'

Millie spent the next two hours indulging in her second-favourite pastime – gossiping about food, ingredients, utensils, old recipes, new recipes, experiments she had tried and scored a fail. If she couldn't spend her time slicing, chopping, beating, whisking, then she wanted to be chewing over new possibilities with someone who shared her passion, like Jen or Poppy. Now she had found herself a culinary soulmate in the Caribbean and her heart, like her hair, ballooned.

Night fell with unexpected haste and in the darkness the humidity took on a velvety texture. The silhouette of Gros Piton presented an eerie, almost menacing presence, and the town scattered at its base sparkled with myriad amber lights. Out in the bay, tiny specks of light danced on the surface of the waves as the yachts and schooners entertained parties of tourists with barbeques, live calypso music and locally produced rum.

The toot of a horn sounded from the courtyard.

'Ah, that'll be Henri.'

It hadn't occurred to Millie until that moment that she would be spending the night on the hillside alone. From what she could see, the villa had no immediate neighbours. She shoved the unsettling thought of her isolation in an unfamiliar country deep into the crevices of her mind.

Ella gathered Millie into her arms and deposited a kiss on each of her cheeks.

'Now, it's all arranged. Tomorrow morning, I plan on introducing you to the delights of Castries market. You need to touch, squeeze, sniff, as well as taste the sensational produce we St Lucians take for granted before we begin to test out their ability to merge with the spices in our recipes. I've sorted out your transport. Oh, I just know that the Paradise Cookery School is going to be amazing! I can't wait to get started.'

Ella collected her huge canvas handbag and bustled off to the tiny red Fiat, which sped away down the hill before Millie could catch a glimpse of its driver.

Chapter Four

Millie opened the door to her balcony and blinked into the sunlight. Despite her initial fear of being alone on the hillside, she had slept from the moment her head hit the pillowcase; a combination of exhaustion, jet lag and the tranquillity of the surroundings, not to mention the fact that she was so far away from home and its accompanying problems. She truly believed in the old adage that physical distance offered an alternate perspective.

She showered, washed her hair and ran a splodge of coconut oil through the strands. For her morning saunter around Castries she decided on her navy capri pants and a Breton-striped T-shirt – one of her favourite combinations. Sequinned sandals completed her ensemble with her bug-eyed sunglasses perched on the top of her head and trusty straw bag slung over her shoulder. She was eager to familiarize herself with the local produce, the fruit and vegetables, as well as gauge the availability of freshly caught seafood. Her brain bulged with a myriad of possibilities to add to her recipe scrap box.

Millie skipped down the stairs and into the courtyard, surprised to see an unfamiliar vehicle waiting for her. She opened the passenger door.

'Hi! I'm Millie... Oh, it's you.'

'Well, I *had* expected a barrage of effusive thanks for giving up my morning to drive you to Castries, but I suppose I should have known better,' said Zach, rolling his eyes. 'Henri couldn't make it – some emergency or other at the newspaper. Ella says she'll meet you at the market. She grabbed a lift with her friend Denise – the other half of the village gossip-vine.'

'Great, thanks. Yes, it's very kind of you.'

Millie jumped into the passenger seat, but as she slammed the door shut one of her sandals dropped from her toes. Zach was so swift off the mark that they had reached the end of the driveway before she had time to shriek for him to stop. With her face flushed with embarrassment, she scrambled from the SUV, hobbled back up the hill to collect her flip-flop, and resumed her seat next to him, unable to meet his eyes.

To add to her mortification, Zach burst into raucous laughter, shaking his head as though he couldn't believe what had just happened.

'Okay. It wasn't that funny!' Millie snapped, turning her face away from him to look out of the window.

'Well, not if you don't possess a sense of humour!' Zach revved the engine, gripped the steering wheel and, still chuckling, set off down the hill.

'Are you always this irritating or do you save up your insults and deliver them all at once?'

'You know, there's just something about you, Little Miss Clumsy, that brings out the comedy in every situation. You must have spent years honing the skill, eh?'

Millie decided that Zach's rudeness did not warrant a reply and that silence was preferable to engaging him in a conversation he obviously thought passed as wit. She clutched her bag to her chest and sank down into her seat, hoping he would get the message. Thankfully, he was too busy concentrating on navigating the twists and bends of the only road that led to the Caribbean island's capital than on his mission to wind her up until she snapped.

They shot past tiny hamlets of no more than a dozen houses, each painted in a different hue – canary yellow, fiery red and green, cobalt blue – some pristine with well-kept gardens, others in need of a fresh coat of paint, all with the most magnificent, uninterrupted view of the sea. Fields crammed with the island's staple crops of banana, coconut and mango lined both sides of the road, interspersed with palm trees and cocoa plantations, until they dropped down to the coast and the scenery became more urban.

'You'll love Castries. You should try to see a bit more of the town than just the food market, though.'

An unpleasant thought suddenly occurred to her and before she could stop herself she had blurted, 'You're not coming with us, are you?'

'Now here I was thinking you would jump at the chance for someone to carry your bags!'

Millie glowered at Zach, causing him to laugh again. 'Don't worry. My instructions are to drop you off at the market and leave. Henri will meet you after lunch to give you and Ella a lift back to the villa when you're ready.'

Zach slowed down to almost a walking pace as they approached the outskirts of the capital and the roads became tight with traffic. To Millie's eyes, Castries presented a shabby, worn-out vibe; several houses and shops were in desperate need of repair, with rusting oil drums and broken-up vehicles in their yards and mangy dogs roaming amongst the scattered detritus of city life. A brigade of teenage youths loitered outside a roadside bar, cigarettes dangling from their lips, passing round a bottle of home-brewed rum.

'Okay, Princess Pout, your ordeal is over. We're here.'

Millie couldn't get out of her seat fast enough. She muttered thanks, then slammed the passenger-side door with a resounding thud and stalked away without saying goodbye. What had she done to deserve this onslaught of mockery? Next time she would insist on calling a taxi. Even if she had to walk up the hill in the daily deluge of liquid sunshine, it was better than being subjected to Zach's personal brand of humour at her expense.

Castries market presented a kaleidoscope of local produce. Every stall was stacked with the best St Lucian horticulture had to offer. All around her Millie found inspiration; from the abundance of fresh fruit and salad vegetables, to the herbs and spices for the sauces and flavourings she was keen to experiment with. She spotted Ella and Denise lingering over a basket of mangoes and they gestured her over. They squeezed and sniffed the flesh – neither overripe nor underripe – perfect. Millie snatched up a curved fruit that looked like a green banana, exclaiming at her amazing discovery as though she had never set eyes on such magnificence before.

'Do you know what that is, Millie?' asked Denise, indicating the green fruit Millie was waving in the air.

Millie searched her jet-lagged brain for the name of the banana-like object but couldn't drag it from its slumber.

'Well, I know it's not an underripe banana,' she laughed, running her fingers through a basket of fresh cinnamon sticks and inhaling the aroma that screamed Christmas.

The two childhood friends smiled, clearly enjoying their role as gastronomic guides of the picturesque market that teemed with locals and tourists alike. The intoxicating fragrance of nutmeg, vanilla, mango and jasmine rippled through the air, so thick with humidity that Millie thought she could slice it into segments and serve it with a splodge of mascarpone – and perhaps a dribble of her favourite amaretto added for flavour.

'It's plantain – we eat it pan-fried in a dollop of butter and sprinkled with soft brown sugar and cinnamon. It features in lots of Caribbean recipes, along with sweet potatoes, cassava, dasheen and okra.'

The three women moved on to the next stall, greeting the proprietor with an enquiry into her husband's health. The tabletop was heaped with pyramids of multicoloured spices and bunches of freshly cut herbs – some Millie recognized, others were unfamiliar. She stuck the tip of her finger into a paprika-like powder and touched it to the tip of her tongue. A myriad of flavours burst into her mouth and her brain whirred with possibilities – fish, *tick*, lamb, *tick*, courgettes, *tick*, bitter chocolate soufflé, *tick*…

Next, they chatted to a fisherman about his daily catch of seafood, landed fresh in Castries harbour that morning. Tuna, swordfish, red snapper and shark, all fought for prominence alongside lobster, crab and shrimp. Then came a stall crammed with examples of local craftwork – wooden carvings, woven shopping bags and baskets, garish souvenirs and T-shirts, hand-crafted jewellery.

As the early afternoon heat intensified, the market throng thinned to housewives contemplating that evening's supper and restaurant owners bartering for a good price. A smattering of tourists sat on the wall outside, cooling down with a fresh globe of coconut water or indulging in a lunch carton of dorado in tangy Creole sauce topped with tomatoes, onions and mashed green figs, swilling it down with the tart, green mango juice on offer from a sun-shrivelled gentleman at the entrance to the market.

Millie could have spent all day meandering the market pathways, questioning the vendors, fingering the intricately carved masks and brightly coloured scarves and kaftans. The sun smiled down on their shopping expedition and the conversation flowed easily as she chatted about her job at the patisserie and her excitement at being involved in Claudia's brand-new venture.

'It's going to be a push to achieve a fully functioning kitchen in time for the arrival of the wedding students, you know,' Ella said to Denise, surreptitiously casting a glance at Millie's face for her reaction.

'I'm sure it'll be okay, Ella,' said Millie, with more optimism than she felt. 'As long as all the appliances, cabinets and worktops are with us on Monday morning and the tradesmen start work straight away, we should finish on time. Although, we might still be cleaning the floors when the first guests arrive.'

Ella and Denise exchanged looks and a soupçon of anxiety gnawed at Millie's abdomen.

'What?'

'Oh, nothing. Don't mind us.'

Ella took Millie's arm and guided her through the narrow alleyways of Castries to a tiny restaurant, no more than a wooden shack, squeezed in between a barber's shop and an Irish-themed bar. A group of elderly men lounged in the shade on the pavement in red plastic chairs, putting the world to rights around a bottle of rum.

'Let's get some lunch.'

A huge platter of food appeared as if by magic – she wasn't even aware they had ordered. Stuffed red snapper finished with a flourish of thyme and lemon balm, a timbale of fragrant rice and a tangy mango salad – a mixture of spring onions, red and green peppers, cucumber and fresh basil. The meal produced a delicious symphony on the tongue and her taste buds zinged with appreciation.

'Here, try some of this,' offered Denise, holding a silver spoon aloft.

'Mmm,' said Millie, licking her lips.

'It's green bean salad – onions, sweetcorn, red peppers with a dressing of soy sauce, thyme, garlic, chilli and a hint of lemon juice. And wait until you try the roasted sweetcorn spread with butter whipped with fresh coconut.'

They polished off lunch, washed down with a jug of fresh, home-made lemonade, and Ella ordered a chocolate mousse.

'What do you think?'

Millie dug in her spoon and wrapped her tongue around the sweet, smooth dessert. The flavour was velvety yet bitter. When she allowed the mousse to slip down her throat she gasped as an intense heat invaded her mouth and she had to take a glug of her lemonade.

The women burst into laughter, delighted at her reaction.

'What is this?'

'It's Michael's special recipe – a family secret, I'm afraid. Of course, the main ingredient is fiery red chilli,' chuckled Ella. 'Goes well with dark chocolate, don't you think?'

'I think his hand slipped preparing this batch!'

A sudden scraping of chairs on the pavement warned Millie it was three o'clock and the daily downpour was imminent. Right on cue the raindrops arrived, smashing down from the sky with a ferocity she had never encountered on the streets of London, or Oxford for that matter. It was as though the sluice gates of heaven had opened, tipping the contents onto the unsuspecting ants milling around down below.

They lingered over tiny cups of black coffee, which tasted to Millie like rancid petrol – same consistency, same appearance. They chatted about favourite family recipes, new ingredients that had become fashionable, whilst watching the continuous slap of rain on the tarmac outside. They shared their respective childhood aspirations, which for all three of them, had inevitably centred around the preparation and consumption of food.

'It's only now, in my sixth decade, that I've come to understand that food is more than just a compound with which to replenish the body. That to savour the exquisite flavours on the tongue is akin to a lover tasting his sweetheart's lips for the first time,' Denise mused.

Millie had never forgotten that first sweet infusion in her veins of the beginnings of a lifelong passionate relationship with the culinary arts; the dream to be fortunate enough to make it her living, a career which she could enjoy and not feel it was work, never moan about the monotony of routine – for a chef there was never such a complaint. Every day, every recipe, every ingredient presented a different challenge, one which taxed not only the brain and the nimblest of touches, but the heart and the extent of her passion.

'I love to see the smile on diners' lips as they curl the tip of their tongue around a spoon or a fork and then the look on their faces as the flavours burst onto their taste buds. That is my all-consuming passion – to witness the delight in others over something I have created.'

Why had she given all that up to run away to London to work in a tiny patisserie? But, of course, she knew the answer and had no intention of going there. The science behind the melding of ingredients to produce ecstasy had always fascinated Millie. Or it had until recently when she had felt paralysed by misery and shame. But she enjoyed working in the café with Poppy at her side and the return to hard work proved to be the sanctuary she needed. Whipping up a soufflé or a meringue made her happy – that fleeting emotion so pursued by humans in its many guises, like the holy grail of existence. However, reality always lurked in the wings, waiting to push its unwelcome nose into her fantasies.

Millie glanced out of the restaurant's colourful shutters. The downpour had freshened the oppressive humidity and allowed her the chance to breathe in the crisp freshness of cooler air before the onslaught of tropical heat resumed its dominance.

'You've chosen one of the wettest months to come to St Lucia,' said Denise as she dumped three heaped teaspoons of demerara sugar into her second cup of coffee.

'Typical,' said Millie, rolling her eyes at her new friend.

'Ah, here's my Henri.' Ella rose from her seat to greet her son with a bear hug and place two noisy kisses on his cheeks. 'How are Leon and Travis?'

'Leon's exhausted – but that's what studying for your sergeant's exams does to you. He's already talking about the changes he intends to make when he's in charge of the police station in Soufrière. Heaven help the criminal fraternity!'

'Always was ambitious that Leon Hamilton, just like his father,' said Ella. 'What about Travis? How's his foray into wood carving progressing?'

'Not sure about his woodcarving but he got two new commissions for his artwork last month from a Swedish guy who's just bought a place over in Rodney Bay. Wants an oil-on-canvas of the Pitons for his den and a smaller pastel piece for his kitchen. Business at his gallery is brisk, he says. He's worried about Carlton, though.'

'And so he should be,' snapped Denise, slurping the dregs of her coffee as she collected her straw shopping bag and tucked escaped tendrils of curls into her headscarf. 'That boy's a menace.'

Ella raised her eyebrows to her son in question but, wisely perhaps in the presence of Denise, Henri remained silent.

They left the café and sauntered through the streets together, dodging puddles and a battalion of stray cats quenching their thirst whilst they could. The air smelled of coconut oil, fried fish and relaxation, causing Millie's spirits to increase a further notch.

'Okay,' said Denise. 'I've still got a few things left on my shopping list. See you next Saturday, Ella, and make sure you keep those idle builders on their toes.'

Denise left them, tutting and shaking her head as she trotted on her kitten heels down a narrow alleyway between two beach-side shacks, her ample backside rocking in tune to the calypso music spilling out onto the pavement from the bars.

Henri rolled his eyes at his mother's best friend and Ella tapped his arm. 'She means well.'

'Oh, yes, Auntie Dennie may have a heart of gold, but her armoury is diamond-tipped.'

They arrived at his dilapidated Fiat and piled in. It was a squeeze, especially with the plethora of shopping bags Millie and Ella had managed to amass during their trip around the market. A lexicon of recipes was already swirling around Millie's brain and the familiar curl of excitement burst into the pit of her stomach as she contemplated getting started on triple-testing Claudia's chocolate recipes as well as experimenting with her exotic purchases in her tiny kitchen above the garage.

Chapter Five

They left the sprawl of the town behind them and headed south along the coast towards Soufrière. With the infinite expanse of the Caribbean Sea on their right and the aquamarine of the sky above, the scenery on the journey back was picture-postcard perfect. Not a cloud marred its perfection. A cool breeze streamed through the car windows, licking the tips of Millie's ears and lifting the fringe from her forehead. Coupled with the soft sound of reggae on the stereo, she felt her eyes begin to droop until Henri swerved heavily to avoid a cyclist and she tumbled to her right, knocking her temple on the door handle.

'Oww!'

'Sorry, I should have warned you. These roads are lethal.'

Millie swallowed a slug of water, allowing the liquid to trickle slowly down her throat. She turned her face to the breeze and stared at the twin peaks of the Pitons rearing up out of the sea in the distance like the spines of a sleeping dinosaur. Lowering her gaze, she had to blink to make sure she wasn't hallucinating. Anchored at the base of Gros Piton was an old galleon-style sailing ship at full mast, flying the Jolly Roger flag.

'Hey, look, pirates!' Millie exclaimed before she could stop herself. Then she giggled – obviously they weren't pirates.

'No, just tourists, although I suppose they are the modern-day equivalent,' said Henri, laughing. 'That's the Unicorn. The owners use her for excursions, treasure hunts and, sometimes, mock battles. She even played a starring role in *Pirates of the Caribbean*!'

Henri glanced across to the passenger seat where his mother snoozed, her head lolling from side to side as he navigated the bends, her cheery face serene in repose.

'Actually, it's the drug smugglers who are the modern scourge of the Caribbean,' said Henri, gripping the steering wheel until his knuckles bleached white. 'And things are getting worse for us in St Lucia, not better. Cocaine gangs are rediscovering the old routes up the eastern Caribbean and I'm worried about what the future will bring.'

'I thought South and Central America were the major problem,' said Millie, her interest piqued.

'Sadly, that's changing. I'm a journalist and I've reported on all sorts of news items for the *Soufrière Tribune*, but in my spare time I've been researching an extensive thesis on the activities of the drug cartels over the last five years – ever since I got back from France where I studied for my degree. They call it the 'balloon effect' – when one drug route is squeezed, a bulge simply emerges elsewhere. Now that the authorities are closely monitoring the airspace of South America and starting to make inroads into the transit of supply over Central America, the frequency and size of the seizures in the Caribbean has tripled.'

Millie noticed the frown on Henri's face as he concentrated on the twisting road ahead but his thoughts were clearly elsewhere.

'It's smaller but more frequent "jumps" are being made now – a "micro-trafficking evolution" they call it. All the old routes used back in the eighties have re-emerged. The drugs are loaded onto "go-fast" speedboats and taken up to the eastern Caribbean islands to St Vincent, St Lucia, Martinique. There're lots of crafts in the waters round here – yachts, fishing boats, ferries, commercial ships with exports such as bananas bound for the US and Europe. Sadly, our customs department is more lax than in the US and the UK, for instance, and some of it's getting through. It's the suffering of the families that upsets me more than anything, though.'

Henri paused to draw in a deep steadying breath, his expression reflecting his passion about the negative effects this global menace was having on his community.

'So what *are* the authorities doing to stem the flow?'

'The law-enforcement agencies here are doing a very difficult job in economically strained circumstances. They've increased coastal surveillance, improved human and electronic intelligence and detected illicit planes in our airspace. Drug smuggling and money laundering are big business and awash with easy bribes, especially potent in a country that has a high youth-unemployment problem and entrenched poverty. There's corruption too. Salaries are relatively low compared with what the drug barons can pay. And the gangs are violent; drugs flow in, but so do guns for the protection of their precious merchandise and sometimes the drug violence spills over into the local communities.'

Henri's eyes hardened. 'The gangs have no fear, no scruples. Life is cheap. Crimes are committed in broad daylight in front of families and children.

The only talent they exhibit is cruelty. Greed is an insatiable mistress. These men would sell their grannies for a few dollars.'

Henri's shoulders relaxed as he looked across at his mother still snoozing in the sunshine. 'What we need is increased investment in youth employment and training to counteract the lure of the easy money offered by the drugs trade. But it's a multi-layered problem. Cocaine use is not a huge issue in St Lucia, but marijuana is, especially amongst the younger generation. There are large sectors of idle young people with limited skill sets to provide for their daily upkeep. The police maintain a zero tolerance of cannabis use, so they may spend a brief period in jail, which causes them to descend further into the criminal lifestyle. The inevitable stigma attached to being labelled a criminal makes it even harder to find work and often they are disowned by their families. What chance do they have?'

'And is what you're doing at the *Tribune* to highlight the problem working?'

'Sadly, we are like ants fighting a rabid dog. Only if we work together, in numbers, will we stand any chance of being successful. There should be more emphasis on education about drugs in schools, more involvement between parents, teachers and mentors from local businesses. Kids need direction, especially when they don't get it from home.'

Henri averted his eyes and paused before mumbling, 'And many of them do not have the benefit of a male role model in the household to emulate.'

Millie had a sudden impulse to reach out and touch Henri's hand, but she resisted. In profile, he possessed a strong, confident tilt of his chin with a smattering of trendy stubble, but his chocolate-brown eyes, so like his mother's, held sadness. However, his eyelashes instilled a twinge of jealousy in Millie; long, curled and dark, drawing the onlooker into the depths of his soul. She knew Henri's father wasn't around and she didn't want to press him on his upbringing.

As it happened, she didn't have to.

'Mum won't mind me telling you this, but my father has never been a part of my life either. Things were tough when I was growing up, but we managed. I owe her everything for keeping me from succumbing to the scourge of marijuana, or worse, like so many of my contemporaries have.'

Henri paused, his mind adrift on the wings of difficult memories. Millie glanced across at her new friend, taking in the stubborn determination apparent in his clenched jaw and the strength with which he gripped the steering wheel and studiously avoided meeting her eyes. She decided it was time to grasp the conversation baton from Henri and share a little of her own story with him.

'My parents gave me and my sister, Jen, a happy, carefree childhood in a small village in Provence where my mother grew up, before moving to the suburbs in Oxford, and I make sure I count my good fortune every day. But when Dad died, I forgot about all the good things I'd had and concentrated solely on my grief and sorrow over his loss. Why couldn't death have stalked a worthier prey? I used to ask of anyone prepared to listen.'

Millie felt the familiar tightening at her throat as she spoke about her father but found she was able to hold back her tears and continue with their conversation.

'When Mum left to go back home to France, Jen and I decided that we wanted to stay in Oxford. After my training, I landed a fabulous position in a restaurant and met a great guy... well, I thought he was. I thought that with Luke by my side, I could dream of a future where I could allow myself to smile and laugh and not feel guilty. I still think about Dad every day, but with the support of good friends I've finally turned the page on my grief.'

Although it was painful, she thought of the time she had spent with Luke, grateful for the way he had challenged her tendency to wallow in her sadness and urged her to tread the path towards healing. It was ironic that he had also been the person who had sent her reeling back to square one. But she wasn't ready to share that horror story with Henri quite yet.

The town of Soufrière appeared before them, red-tiled roofs, brightly painted shutters and verandas, dogs roaming the gutters in search of a discarded morsel for dinner. Ella woke from her doze and Henri slowed down to navigate the bustling streets of the popular town, threading the car skilfully through the tourists spilling out from the colourful shops and bars.

'I'll jump out here, Henri, if you don't mind,' said Ella as they came to a standstill outside Alisha's Souvenirs. 'See you at dinner tonight. You're welcome to join us, Millie? It would be lovely to have your company.'

'Thanks, Ella, but I'm still working on my jet lag. I would be dreadful company. I'll catch up with you on Monday.'

'Why don't we all meet for cocktails at the Purple Parrot tomorrow?' suggested Henri.

Ella rolled her eyes. 'No, thanks. I've got enough to do getting the recipes for the cookery classes organized. But you should go, Millie. I told you, Andrew makes a mean rum cocktail.'

'Thanks, Ella, I will. I'll see you on Monday morning then. You *will* be there when the kitchen fitters arrive, won't you?'

'Sure.'

Millie waved her off before Henri continued their journey. She didn't want to acknowledge the nerves that spun around her stomach when she thought about dealing with a gang of Caribbean workmen. Issuing orders, directing tasks, pointing out snags had never been her forte. But she knew Ella would possess no such reticence. Their schedule was tight and she hoped they would deliver on time without any need for her to flex her recalcitrant authority.

'Thanks for driving me up the hill.' Millie smiled at Henri as he pulled up outside the villa.

After their conversation on the way home she felt they had connected. They occupied the same wavelength on a diverse range of issues and she was comfortable in his company. Maybe it was because of their French genes. There was definitely chemistry between them. It had nothing to do with sexual desire – that was not on the agenda – and she felt even more of an affinity with him for it.

'No problem, Millie. It's been great to show off a small part of our island. Sorry I droned on about the drugs issue but it's something that boils my blood. My best friend Leon, who is a police officer in Soufrière, is a potent source of reliable information. It's my intention to co-publish my academic paper with a former university professor when I've finalized my research. I'm hoping it will attract attention and therefore some funding.'

Millie smiled at him as she opened the car door. 'See you tomorrow at the Purple Parrot.'

'Three o'clock on the dot!' Henri called, waving from the window until his tail lights disappeared around the bend at the bottom of the drive.

Twilight tickled the tops of the palm trees. The Pitons had taken on a dark, sinister aura as fissures of apricot and amber spread over their flanks and the sky above swiftly turned an inky blue. However, the air was still humid and she didn't feel like retiring to her studio bedroom just yet, despite the dragging exhaustion in her bones.

She strolled to the villa's veranda and flicked on the pool's backlights, which glowed beneath the surface like industrial-sized diamonds. She slipped off her sandals, peeled off her shorts and plunged into its cool embrace in her T-shirt. The water slid over her skin like silk and, with an audience of squawking parrots as encouragement, she swam until her muscles burned with the unexpected exertion. She clung to the edge of the pool, staring down at the town nestled at the bottom of the hill, its lights twinkling next to the calm, coal-black sea – a rippling mirror reflecting the ivory orb of the moon. Peace pressed its blanket of comfort to her ears, broken only by the chirp of the cicadas and the buzz of a solitary motorcycle engine as it strained to overcome the gradient.

She dragged her limbs from the water and shook away the droplets of water. Slipping her toes into her sandals and stepping back into her shorts, she padded down the garden path, switching on the outdoor lights as she went. The evening's humidity triggered a veil of mist to rise from the earth like dry ice at an eighties disco. Dragging her hair from her face, she caught a faint whiff of the coconut conditioner she had used that morning in the hope of taming the frizz. She surrendered to the inevitable hair disaster and pressed on with her mission in the hope that her sacrifice of sartorial vanity would lead to the satisfaction of her curiosity.

To her right, just behind the garage complex, stood a large clay oven, which had been painted in a rich ochre. Millie assumed this was where Claudia roasted the cocoa beans she harvested. She arrived at the edge of the plantation where cliques of birds and butterflies peppered the air with the flutter of their tropical wings, and squinted through the descending gloom. The subsequent rows of the cocoa palms melted into a liquid mirage beyond the path. They were the weirdest things she had seen, their fruit growing from their branches like huge warts on a gnarled finger. She ran her fingers over the wrinkled pods, balancing one in the palm of her hand, curious to see what bounty was held within.

She noticed a small machete leaning nonchalantly against one of the trunks next to a woven bamboo basket. She had no idea how long the pods in the wooden crates at the villa's back door had been there, but she craved the chance to dissect a freshly harvested specimen. She weighed the knife in her hand and carefully tapped at the spot where one of the pods joined the tree. It came away easily. She tucked the fruit under her arm and made her way back to the crates on the doorstep, balancing her impromptu harvest on the top of the others ready for its experimental surgery the next day.

Although her T-shirt was completely dry after her swim, perspiration trickled from her temples and between her breasts. As she unlocked the powder-blue door, a harsh wave of exhaustion grabbed at her bones. She locked the door behind her, mounted the stairs and fell onto her cool cotton sheets to enjoy another deep sleep of the jet-lagged.

Chapter Six

When Millie woke the next day the dawn chorus outside her window was well into its second verse. She felt rested and enthusiastic to start experimenting, not only with the ingredients she had purchased at Castries market, but with the cocoa pod she had collected the previous evening. She had a plethora of favourite recipes that included chocolate as an ingredient, and was curious to understand where the beans came from.

She flung back the French doors and inhaled a lungful of the perfumed morning air. It was Sunday and she had the whole morning to herself before she trotted down the hill to check out the Purple Parrot.

She fixed herself coffee and ran her eyes around the tiny kitchen. There was no mistaking that the studio belonged to a professional chef. Every shelf was crammed with a myriad of cookery books; old and more recent, pristine and well-thumbed, thick, heavy tomes and flimsy pamphlets, a cornucopia of brightly coloured gems waiting to be explored, to be freed from the prison of the shelf and their contents brought to life in the kitchen.

Of course, Millie had devoured all of Claudia's published cookery books – over twenty in total – each extolling a unique take on British and European cuisine. Her favourite was *The Baking Blend* – a collection of recipes and reminiscences from Claudia's childhood in Cornwall. She wondered whether Claudia's next book would be a Caribbean-inspired one, or perhaps one that focused solely on chocolate recipes. To Millie, cookery books, like all books, provided a portal into another world: one in which seemingly disparate ingredients could be moulded into taste bud-zinging perfection. Even now, she still experienced the surge of intense pleasure whenever she peeled back a book's cover and ingested the scent of a newly printed page.

Growing up, she had dreamed of becoming a cookery writer. She had rushed home from school after food technology classes, her heart ablaze with a plethora of possibilities for new recipes, which she recorded on pieces of scrap paper scattered around her bedroom. Her teenage self had no reason to believe that her dream would not come true, that life did not always deliver a positive outcome.

She'd developed her obsession with culinary alchemy at the age of seven when her eyes had landed on her aunt's wedding cake, resplendent with a froth of sugar-paste flowers that would have been frowned on today. A monument to melodramatic 1980s taste excess, it had reigned on the top table, drawing her gaze to its suggestion of fantasy like a princess's ballgown more likely to be worn by her sister Jen.

However, intrinsically linked with her enduring desire to emulate the best in the field was the fatal flaw in her plan – her inherent tendency to scatter utensils and ingredients far and wide. She *tried* to be organized, to make lists, to stack jars with the labels facing front, but the hassle just irritated the hell out of her so she ditched the futile attempt and simply reverted to her natural state of dishevelled chaos. She had been born with the clumsy-clutter gene, whilst her sister had been gifted the characteristics of Little Miss Neat and Tidy. She smiled as she recalled the occasion in her teens when she had shoved a bag of caster sugar into her woven raffia shopping basket and left a trail all the way home like Hansel in the forest. But despite the amusement of Jen and her friends, the incident hadn't swayed her one inch from her ambitions. Unlike most childhood dreams, this one did not trickle away at the introduction of Barbie or Blyton or boys.

She had been encouraged in her ambitions by her food tech teacher, Mrs Dovedale, who promised that, if she insisted on pinning her future on the culinary roulette wheel, then she would support her. An angel lurking beneath a battleaxe exterior, Mrs Dovedale spotted a fellow experimentalist in her midst and nurtured Millie's blossoming talent. Millie knew she had her to thank for her career success as she had flunked her more academic subjects. Anyway, what use was being able to quote extensively from Shakespeare or Thomas Hardy if you couldn't master the skills required to feed yourself and your family?

The piles of discarded tomes grew taller as Millie continued her bibliographic archaeology. Eventually she selected one at random – for how could she choose from the kaleidoscope of options? She smoothed her palm over its glossy cover – the face it presented to the world – and selected the first page, inhaling the faint fragrance loitering within of dried dust and printer's ink.

Devouring the contents of a recipe book had always been her go-to therapy whenever her demons invaded, but the best medicine of all was plunging her hands into a bowl of flour or whipping up a soufflé by hand. An idea crept into her mind and she knew immediately how she was going to spend her day. It was what she had been engaged to do anyway.

She extracted her phone and googled information on cocoa production. She found there were several well-known and well-regarded cocoa plantations in the southern area of St Lucia which produced cocoa beans on a commercial scale, unlike Claudia's five acres. She cast her eyes down the listed articles and selected one from the website of a famous chocolate house whose products Jen adored and always requested for her birthday or Christmas gift.

The commentary told her that the Caribbean provided ideal conditions for the precious pods to grow – fertile volcanic soil, high altitudes, heavy rainfall, both sunshine and shade. The trees produced delicate pink-and-white flowers, which matured into the pods she had collected. She learned that one of the reasons cocoa production fell into decline in St Lucia was due to the harvesting being so labour intensive. Each pod had to be carefully selected and cut from the tree so as not to disturb the remaining pods. After they had been split by hand, the beans were removed and allowed to ferment on a bed of banana leaves in wooden boxes, then dried under the Caribbean sun. She was surprised to note that the nibs used to produce the cocoa were inside the bean and not the actual bean itself. It was these nibs that were roasted to a rich, dark brown colour to acquire their chocolatey flavour.

She closed her eyes and was almost able to smell the sweet aroma of her favourite recipes. Further internet searching revealed that she already knew – and something that she repeatedly spouted when challenged over her excessive intake of 'the food of the gods' – chocolate makes you happy! It contains flavonoids and antioxidants, which some research confirmed have anti-ageing properties. One report even went further to extol the benefits of cocoa in extending brain function and memory.

Her academic research over, she turned to her favourite pastime – researching recipes. Just flicking through Claudia's cookbooks for chocolate recipes threw up a myriad of suggestions from the expected to the obscure – from brownies, cookies, cupcakes, to sauces for wild boar and even a mix for a chocolate face mask. Millie could have spent all day subsumed in the pages of cookery advice when real life receded and she could soar away from her problems.

She took a quick inventory of the provisions in the cupboards and the fridge that Claudia had arranged to be delivered before she arrived, and went off in search of her trusty scrap box of recipes. Its contents had been collected over many years from every corner of England and France, jotted on the back of dog-eared theatre programmes, curled-up bus tickets, even napkins and old postcards of St Tropez. She had intended to create a carefully catalogued filing system but somehow it had never materialized, and anyway, her unique version of a Rolodex was a system of sorts. For instance, she knew that the recipe for her mini lemon-curd roulades was on the back of a grease-stained till receipt from Harrods, the ingredients for the chocolate-ganache torte her grandmother used to make were scribbled on an old French Christmas card, and she had no trouble remembering how to rustle up her famous lime-drizzle-and-poppy-seed muffins.

She decided on a batch of her mum's favourite melt-in-the-mouth madeleines, a few mini chocolate-truffle tortes, then maybe some chocolate-and-orange-marmalade cupcakes, taking advantage of the ready availability of the fresh oranges that hung from the trees just outside her window for her home-made marmalade. She also decided it was the perfect opportunity to perform her autopsy on the cocoa pod she had picked the previous night. A curl of excitement wriggled through her chest as she anticipated making a new discovery.

She trotted down the stairs and across the gravelled courtyard to the villa's rear door.

No way! Was she going crazy?

The two scarred wooden crates were still on the whitewashed steps, but they were empty. Not a wrinkled pod in sight – even the solitary specimen she had picked the night before had disappeared.

Yes, okay, she knew she was famous for her clumsiness, her disorganized approach to all things culinary. She accepted that she was messy and forgetful and kept her beloved recipes scrawled on beer mats and receipts in a scrap box. But there was no way she would have dreamed up an entire episode of harvesting a cocoa pod with a machete. And she hadn't allowed a sip of alcohol to pass her lips!

She lifted the lid to peer into the depths of the top crate, which had been lined with a bed of bedraggled banana leaves. A fetid stench reached her nostrils – but there were no cocoa pods. She tried to think how many of the shrivelled rugby balls would have been in each of the crates – probably at least a dozen.

But not one remained. She chanced a glance over her shoulder, peering into the lush palm trees as if she were expecting someone to leap out and shout, 'Surprise!' but of course no one did. She skirted the white-painted veranda to the front of the villa overlooking the serene, undisturbed surface of the pool. She checked the handles of the French doors – locked. There was nothing to indicate anyone had been there. No note, no envelope, no boots by the back door.

She shook her head and rubbed the heels of her palms over her eyes before meandering back to the studio, reasoning that Ella must have dropped by and taken the pods home. But even as she filed the mystery away into her mind's Rolodex, she knew it was an unlikely conclusion to grasp on to. For one thing, Ella didn't drive.

Once back in the kitchen, Millie's spirits lifted, her hands sped up and she baked, baked, baked as though her life depended on it. She creamed the butter and caster sugar for the cupcakes by hand before adding the eggs, flour and a sprinkle of cocoa and grated orange peel, the smell causing her mouth to water. Finally, she divided up the mixture into five muffin trays and slotted them into the oven.

The scent of warm buttery chocolate cake permeated the kitchen and she inhaled the wonderful aroma. She shoved the mixing bowl and cutlery into the sink and turned on the tap. Water spurted everywhere and her crimson vest top was splattered with a random pattern of droplets. She took a moment to survey the kitchen. Flour and cocoa powder scattered every available work surface, interspersed with splodges of butter, slivers of grated chocolate, and how had a smudge of orange marmalade appeared on the freezer door? Every available surface was strewn with implements and she knew she should tidy up as she went along, but that had always been her downfall. Unlike most professional chefs, she preferred to be surrounded by the paraphernalia of cooking, with not only the raw ingredients receiving her undivided attention but also her Kenwood mixer, her copper pans, her Jamie Oliver knives.

Happiness rushing through her veins as she swept her hair away from her face, leaving a trail of flour along her cheek, she turned her attention to making the madeleines. The sweet smell of baking sent her memory scuttling back to her childhood when she and Jen began their mutual love affair with all things cake-related. They had stood on their tiptoes on a wooden stool next to their mother and whisked, beaten and licked to their hearts' content. In her teens, she had been teased for frequently sporting a liberal dusting of flour or icing sugar, and, instead of the latest designer fragrance, a hint of caramelized apples.

The sniggers of her peers had hurt but she had refused to allow it to define her. She was always going to be identified as different by her, albeit faint, French accent and therefore fodder for their adolescent jibes. She'd worked quickly on erasing it and now only a trace could be heard when she was tired, angry or under the influence of a few glasses of cognac when it would become as thick as royal icing on a wedding cake and no doubt impenetrable to the ears of the natives of rural Oxfordshire.

She tested the final batch of cupcakes with a skewer and set them on wire racks to cool, then slid the trays of madeleines into the oven and started on the mini chocolate-truffle tortes. Baking had not only been her secret salvation in her teenage years, but had come to her rescue ever since in times of heartbreak and despair. Over the years at Le Cordon Bleu she grew accustomed to the compliments on her early forays into gastronomic alchemy. The obvious pleasure of hearing her tutors' praise instilled a sweet taste of vanity in her heart and an addiction to its continuance.

Each recipe she tried became more intricate. She would perform meticulous autopsies on pastries purchased from the bakeries dotted along the streets of Oxford, cataloguing each ingredient, recording its ability to interact with its companion, improving them until they became a serenade on the lips. She had even forced herself to memorize the science behind the art of baking in order to pass her exams; no mean feat for a girl who consistently spent her school days daydreaming about the recipes she'd work on once she got home.

She ignored the detritus of culinary labour piling up in the sink and along the countertops and continued with the whirlwind of activity. As she decorated the cupcakes, she couldn't prevent her thoughts flying back to Luke, his dark blue eyes staring into hers in the bedroom they shared above a flower shop, their bodies glistening with perspiration. She knew she should be grateful to him – early on in their relationship he had led her along such an idyllic path that she had truly believed she could come to terms with losing her beloved father. Their relationship had been tempestuous; the sex a revelation. But of course, like everything

in her life, all good things must come to an end –
and boy, did Luke do that in style.

After removing the final tray of miniature
chocolate-truffle tortes, she swept her eyes around
the kitchen – a veritable cascade of chaos. It
looked like a scene from *The Caribbean Bake Off
Massacre*, but on the gastronomic battlefield there
were bound to be casualties. She ran her eyes over
the blobs of marmalade dripping down the front
of the fridge, and the tea towels and dishcloths
slumped amongst the washing-up. Realizing she
was humming a Bob Marley tune, her lips curled
into a smile. She stood back, hands on hips, to
survey the fruits of her toil.

With a jolt of surprise, she realized she
had seriously over-baked. She had made over
fifty madeleines, five dozen chocolate-and-orange-
marmalade cupcakes and a tottering pyramid of
chocolate tortes! Whilst she adored desserts of
every variety, there was no way she was going to
get through all that by herself.

Noticing a long meandering snail's trail of cocoa
on the floor, she fished a cloth from the sink and
knelt down to clean it up, her buttocks high in the
air, wiggling from side to side as she got stuck into
an off-key rendition of 'No Woman, No Cry'. It
was not her *best* angle to present to visitors.

'Hello? Anyone home? Oh, my God, what's happened here? Marmalade Armageddon?'

Chapter Seven

'A bit of an exaggeration, don't you think?'

'I thought all professional chefs were possessed of Poirot-esque fastidiousness in their working environment? With expletives liberally dispensed to minions who step out of line with a whisk?'

'I see you've fallen into the trap of viewing everyone as a Ramsayan cliché,' she countered.

'And do you usually model your culinary creations?' Zach swept his eyes over her hair.

Irritation rose in her chest at the continuation of their ridiculous verbal sparring but she was determined to remain calm and rise above it. She shot into the bathroom where the ornate, gilt-framed mirror confirmed his diagnosis. She was indeed wearing an assortment of the ingredients from her masterpieces. Her blonde hair resembled an ice-speckled pigeon's nest, only it was flour not snow that had provided her with a generous dusting. More embarrassing, however, was the splodge of marmalade on her left cheek. She scrubbed it off with her cuff and smoothed down her fringe.

'Hey, who said you could help yourself?' smirked Millie, as she rejoined Zach who was busy munching his way through a still-warm cupcake, his palm positioned at his chin to catch any escaping morsel.

'Well, you seem to have overestimated your pool of consumers. What do you plan on doing with five dozen cupcakes and a whole brigade of little shell-shaped cakes?'

'They're not "little shell-shaped cakes", they're madeleines.'

Zach grinned mischievously as he helped himself to three.

'Isn't that a little greedy?'

'They're not for me.'

Zach placed his fingers to his lips and gave a short whistle. A whirlwind of black-and-white fluff raced up the stairs and bowled straight across to greet Millie. Taken completely by surprise she stepped backwards, tripped over a bag of sugar she had left on the floor and tumbled onto her buttocks, knocking a glass measuring jug from its precarious position on the draining board onto the tiles. It shattered into four pieces.

'Agh!' She covered her face with her hands as the springer spaniel attempted to lick her cheek clean of its marmalade coating. 'Get off me! Dogs are not allowed in the kitchen!'

'Definitely not an animal lover, then? Is there anything you have an affinity with? If not humans or animals, perhaps plants? No, I'd hazard a guess you are as au fait with the natural environment as I am with whipping up a mango soufflé with raspberry-mint jus. Or are you just permanently grouchy? Come on, Binks, leave the lady alone.'

The dog trotted obediently to Zach's side and sat, his bead-like eyes trained longingly on the madeleines in his owner's hands. Zach took pity on him and tossed one to his best friend before crouching down to offer Millie his palm to help her up.

'For your information, I adore animals. Especially dogs!'

Millie's exasperation with Binks's master gnawed at her chest. Once again she ignored his outstretched hand and pushed herself to standing, whilst Zach scooted round to collect the shards of glass, wrap them in a discarded flour bag and spray the floor with disinfectant. Finally, he tossed another of her madeleines to a grateful Binks.

'They're not dog biscuits, you know.' Millie couldn't understand why Zach's presence made her so tetchy. Maybe it was because everything he said caused her to rise to the bait when he denigrated her character traits. So she couldn't help herself saying, 'And who calls their dog "Binks"? It's a ludicrous name.'

'Oh, I suppose you'd call him "Fluffy" or "Curly", would you?'

Millie had the grace to blush and decided to leave any further character assassination for a more auspicious occasion.

'Coffee?'

'Please.'

She unearthed the kettle from beneath a pile of scrunched-up greaseproof paper and set it to boil.

'So if you won't share your bounty with Binks and me, what do you intend to do with it all? There's enough to feed a ravenous regiment.'

'I hadn't really thought that far ahead.'

She busied herself at the sink so as not to have to look at him. Now that Zach had mentioned it, her morning's baking splurge did seem to be a waste of food. He was so infuriating – why did he have to be right as well?

She slammed down a mug of coffee on the marble worktop in front of him, its contents sloshing onto the surface. Zach calmly tore off a piece of kitchen towel and wiped the spillage away before strolling outside to the balcony.

'Well, if you're sure you don't intend to indulge in a secret cupcake-and-madeleine marathon, I might have an idea what you can do with the products of your impromptu bake off. And you can indulge in a little fun at the same time. You do know what fun is, don't you? Do they have that in the cloudy skies and grim-streaked streets of London?'

'Of course we do!' Millie shot back before realizing that once again Zach had managed to hit the spot with his sarcasm. She most certainly had not had much fun in the capital's hotspots over the last six months as she nursed her broken heart, despite Poppy's constant encouragement. But she wasn't about to admit that to Zach. 'I can party with the best of them.'

She saw Zach smirk as he realized his bullet had been well aimed and had found its mark. However, he was astute enough also to realize that the rising temperature in the room was radiating not from the oven but from the anger bubbling up inside Millie.

'So, Little Miss Cupcake, I propose we take a trip down the hill to see a couple of friends of mine. You'll like Dylan. He runs a diving school on the beach in Soufrière, mainly for a bunch of pale-skinned corporate guys anxious to experience a dose of excitement beneath the waves. It's Sunday lunchtime so I think we can be sure to find him having a beer at the Purple Parrot next door.'

'Great, I'm actually meeting a few friends there at three so that works perfectly.'

Millie wasn't ashamed to admit how much she enjoyed the expression of surprise zip across Zach's handsome face, but he recovered well.

'Okay. Why don't you wrap everything up and slot those perfumed twinkly toes of yours in a pair of flip-flops? We'll hop on my quad bike and deliver these mouth-watering examples of five-star baking to Andrew who owns the Purple Parrot. He can hand them out to his customers as a post-Sunday lunch treat. Every little helps to drum up business. It's a win-win solution. I know Claudia would approve and nothing will be wasted. I'll introduce you to Lottie who works behind the bar. I think you two will get on famously.'

Millie's simmering irritation with Zach was suddenly doused. Perhaps this grouchy guy did possess some redeeming features after all. It was a very generous-spirited answer to her dilemma. She had no problem with the donation of the products of her labour. What she *did* have an issue with was riding on the back of a quad bike with Zach at the wheel. Yet how could she refuse without looking uncharitable and confirming all his suspicions about her? Could she suggest they walked down to the town? Yet how would they carry everything? And where was her courage and her promise to herself to try new things? But, quad biking?

'Fine. Just give me ten minutes.'

'Great, see you in the courtyard. Come on, Binks. I'll drop you off at the lodge.'

Millie busied herself tearing off sheets of grease-proof paper. She wrapped up the chocolate tortes, most of the cupcakes – well, she had to eat something – and half of the madeleines, stashing them in a couple of plastic boxes which she then tied with string so she could hook them over her arm.

Finally, she cast a glance around the kitchen. It was a complete mess. Oh, well, she would tidy up when she got back. She had nothing else to do before the hard work started on the villa's kitchen the next day and she and Ella got stuck into the recipe testing.

She stripped off her flour-covered T-shirt and replaced it with an embroidered kaftan her mother had bought her for her birthday, teaming it with her navy capri pants. She would have preferred to wear heeled sandals, but decided that in this instance practicality should reign over sartorial elegance. She wasn't sure what the dress etiquette was for the back of a quad bike but she hazarded a guess it was not short skirts and stilettos. Finally, she ran a comb through her hair before reluctantly taking the route of least resistance and tying it back with Poppy's hair tie.

She grabbed her baked goodies and trotted down the stairs for her rendezvous with the dreaded mechanical bronco. Unsurprisingly, Zach was already waiting for her, revving the engine. He surveyed her change of clothes and her brightly coloured sequinned flip-flops.

'Hurry up and hop on, Pastry Princess. Unless, of course, you *want* to get caught in the daily downpour?'

Chapter Eight

Millie had ridden a jet ski many times along the sparkling sea of the Côte d'Azur, but never a mud-splattered quad bike. The thought was just too incongruous. The vehicle looked like something a schoolboy had designed for a James Bondesque computer quest. She climbed onto the padded seat, her heart doing its best to escape from her ribcage, her stomach churning in trepidation when she remembered how steep the hill down to Soufrière was.

'Hold on tight!'

Zach pulled away much faster than Millie had expected, forcing her to grab on to his waist or risk somersaulting from the back. As she clung on for dear life, she could feel the tautness of his muscles through his flimsy cotton T-shirt and a ripple of something she hadn't felt in months meandered through her lower abdomen and sent heat to her cheeks. She had never been so grateful to be occupying the rear seat.

Telling herself she was assisting with the aerodynamics, she scooted closer to Zach, moulding her body to his. She was surprised at how perfect a fit they were as she relished the whiff of his citrussy cologne in the oncoming breeze that caused her senses to fizz.

'Are you okay?'

'I'm fine, thanks,' Millie replied, a smile tugging her lips.

'Do you think you could loosen your grip a little then? I'm not a fan of medieval torture and your fingernails are sharp enough to be pressed into service on a bed of nails!'

'Oh, sorry!'

Millie relaxed her grasp and instead of dwelling on the unfamiliar reaction she had just experienced to Zach's proximity, she concentrated her attention on the way the afternoon sun washed the dark volcanic triangles of the Pitons in a golden hue, producing a frame of fire for their beauty.

They arrived in Soufrière a few minutes later and she heaved a sigh of relief when she dismounted in the town's main street, a corridor of vibrant Caribbean entertainment no matter what the browser's preference. Restaurants and cafés fought for space with souvenir shops and excursion vendors; chapels of consumerism designed to tempt the unwary into parting with their holiday dollars. Tourists spilled out from the beachside bars, swaying their hips to the calypso and reggae rhythms, safe in the knowledge that the office would not beckon the next day.

Nestled at the far end of the main street was the Purple Parrot. Its thatched roof and wide-open shutters were exactly as Millie had expected. The door was ajar, and, as she stepped inside, the scent of the sweet hibiscus that dangled like a lei garland around the eaves floated into her nostrils. At the rear, the bar's wooden veranda led directly onto the beach and was set with an eclectic collection of tables and chairs. Diners lingered over their freshly ground coffees and exotic cocktails whilst other patrons had removed their shoes and taken to the sand to dance to the muted virtuoso of sounds rippling from the speakers on the steps.

A young couple had ventured as far as the waves, shoving each other closer and closer into the froth of the ebb and flow, alternately laughing and shrieking with objection as they dashed away from an inevitable soaking.

'Come on. I'll introduce you to Andrew.'

Zach guided Millie to the bar where the proprietor of the Purple Parrot was shaking a cocktail as if auditioning for a starring role in a Tom

Cruise movie. His eyes constantly flicked around the room; clearly a man with an ingrained habit of checking his diners' needs. His lined face cracked into a smile when he spotted them approaching.

'Hey, Zach! Great to see you, man… and your girlfriend.' He wiped his palms on the front of his chef's whites before grabbing Millie's fingers and raising them to his lips. 'Landed yourself a beauty this time.'

Millie saw Zach roll his eyes. Clearly this was a well-worn routine between the friends. 'Andrew, this is Amelia Harper. She's here to help set up the Paradise Cookery School for Claudia. She's brought you an abundance of delicious pastries to distribute to your lucky customers – free of charge. Oh, and be nice to her. No teasing – she's French.'

'Ignore him. I'm actually half French. What's the problem with being French, anyway?' She shot Zach a withering look but he was busy opening the boxes of cakes and missed it. 'Please, call me Millie. It's good to meet you, Andrew.'

'Manic Millie here had a feverish frenzy in the kitchen this morning and seriously overestimated her appetite. Couldn't let all these goodies go to waste. There's probably over a hundred chocolate cupcakes in here.'

'Wow,' exclaimed Andrew. 'Thank you very much. They smell divine. Do you think we should we give them a taste-test first?'

'Great idea! We wouldn't want to risk poisoning your clientele, especially in these economically difficult times,' smirked Zach.

Andrew shook his head before turning his attention back to Millie. 'It's really kind of you, Millie. Thanks again.'

'No problem.'

'Can you squeeze us in for lunch, Andy? You look slammed.'

Andrew's jawline tightened and his mahogany eyes narrowed. 'Marc hasn't turned up yet. It's the second time this week he's missed a shift. Why don't you grab a table on the veranda and I'll send Lottie over to take your order when she's finished mooning over Dylan. Oh, and Zach? Don't forget to introduce Millie to one of my signature cocktails!'

Andrew allowed a faint twist of his lips to soften his features as he thrust his red bandana higher up his forehead to push back his ebony curls from his face. Clearly, he wore the kerchief as a symbol of his celebrity chef hipness, but it didn't work and served only to emphasize his tired, crumpled features. He strode back into the kitchen to supervise the cooking.

Millie followed Zach to a table overlooking the dappled sands of Soufrière beach. They turned their heads in unison as a shriek of laughter pierced the air and a young girl came flying towards the steps, sand scattering in her slipstream, her long magenta locks tossed high above her head like a wild Medusa as she tried to escape from the guy chasing her. He caught her by the waist and they fell together onto the beach where they proceeded to roll like a pair of anorexic sumo wrestlers.

'Lottie! Put Dylan down! We could do with some service over here,' Zach laughed, before lowering his voice to Millie. 'Another gap-year lingerer. As you can see, Lottie not only appreciates the stunning Caribbean scenery and the laid-back lifestyle we have in abundance in St Lucia, but also enjoys playing the lead role in her own personal romcom with our resident beach guy.'

The couple leapt up the wooden treads to join Zach and Millie. After introductions, Lottie floated off into the bar to collect the tray of cocktails Andrew had prepared whilst she had been on her break. She delivered them with a wide smile to the group of diners who were clearly on their fourth or fifth sampling of the Purple Parrot's legendary beverage.

'Great to meet you, Millie. I'm Dylan. I own the diving school over there.'

Dylan proudly indicated the ramshackle shed at the far side of the restaurant where surfboards, dinghies and wetsuits had been crammed into a wire cage sealed with two huge barn doors painted with a flag of sunflower yellow, crimson and green. A rusted hand-painted sign declared it to be 'Dylan's Dive Shack'.

'Fancy a trip out in the boat whilst you're here? The reef is spectacular, we're right next to the marine reserve. I can guarantee you'll get close up and personal with turtles, octopus and parrotfish, maybe even a seahorse or two.'

'I'd love to, thanks, Dylan. Maybe next week, though. I want to get the kitchen renovations at the villa under way as soon as possible. Claudia's relying on me to make sure everything is perfect and delivered on schedule. I think I might have my work cut out.'

'Ah, yes, I heard Claudia was setting up an upmarket culinary experience. Good luck to her.'

Dylan dropped down into one of the mismatched wooden chairs and accepted a cold Red Stripe from Lottie before she plonked a huge, goldfish bowl of a cocktail glass in front of Millie, its rim dipped in green-dyed sugar crystals and sporting an umbrella, a slice of lime and a scatter of mint leaves.

'One Purple Parrot Mojito! Enjoy.'

Millie took a tentative sip, allowing the flavours to dance on her tongue before swallowing. Within seconds the alcohol burned at her throat and she gasped at its strength, just about managing not to succumb to a fit of coughing.

Dylan chuckled. 'I'd take it easy with that magician's potion, Millie. It's made with fifty-per-cent-proof rum. I don't know where Andrew sources that stuff but it's lethal.'

Dylan ran his fingers through his tufted hair, the colour of summer honey, and scratched at his short sandy beard. He leaned back on his chair's legs and tipped the remnants of his beer in his mouth, his T-shirt rising upwards to display an impressive six-pack above his frayed denim shorts. Millie noticed his biceps were firm too, no doubt gained by lugging heavy diving equipment and dragging boats up and down the beach, not from boring, repetitive sessions spent at an indoor gym. Tiny wisps of fair hair curled up his tanned forearms and sent a surprise spasm of pleasure down her spine.

'How long have you lived in Soufrière, Dylan?' Millie asked, chancing another taste of her cocktail. She was enjoying his easy company, the diametric opposite of the snippy conversations she was forced to endure with Zach. It was like being with Robinson Crusoe's brother. The leather thong tied around his neck held a polished shark tooth and a silver charm she couldn't make out. Colourful string bracelets encircled his wrists and his skin glowed with the golden hue of someone who spends most of their day in the sunshine.

'Came to St Lucia on a gap year after uni ten years ago. The ex-pat community here is a crockpot of beach bums, rat-race escapees, bankrupts and love cheats. This paradise winds its way under your skin and into your heart without you noticing. Couldn't bear to go back to rain-soaked Manchester, so I stayed. Already had my PADI licence and Dad re-mortgaged his house so I could buy the Shack. I owe him big time!'

'What does your dad think of St Lucia? He must be proud you've made such a success of the business.' Millie saw a cloud float across Dylan's pale blue eyes for the first time.

'He's never made the trip out. I've pleaded, cajoled, threatened. Even bought the guy a return ticket last summer but he gave it to my mate Carl.'

Dylan snagged another Red Stripe from Lottie as she passed their table. She slapped his hand away but her eyes held such deep affection it was obvious to even the casual onlooker that she adored him. The girl radiated youthful expectation. Life had not yet had sufficient opportunity to squeeze the optimism lodged within.

'Since Mum died he's refused to step out of his comfort zone, or do anything really, except go to work and pay the bills. She's been gone ten years but still he won't entertain meeting anyone for a drink, even as friends. He's as handsome as I am,' continued Dylan with a mischievous wink. 'So he's definitely not short of offers, but he still loves Mum.'

'He's promised to come out this summer, hasn't he?' said Zach. 'To name the boat.'

'Dad put up the cash to buy us a new dive boat, too.' Dylan pointed with the neck of his beer bottle to the sleek white boat moored at the wooden jetty outside the diving school. Millie could just about make out the vessel's name – *Nigella's Navette*. 'We named it after Mum, so he can't refuse to launch it with a bottle of bubbly in her honour, can he? I'm not holding my breath, though.'

Dylan tipped his chair back onto all fours again, banged down his empty bottle on the table and jumped to his feet.

'Great to meet you, Millie. Catch you later, Zach,' and he fist-bumped his friend before sauntering off down the main street, Lottie's eyes scorching a hole in his back.

'Another mojito, Millie?'

'Gosh, no way! I can hardly see straight as it is. Thanks, though.'

'What about an Andy's Blast? It's made with the flesh from the cocoa pods grown on the hills surrounding Soufrière – delicious. You've got to try one. I won't take no for an answer.'

Lottie trotted off to the bar to juggle the spirits. She took such care in the drink's preparation it was as though the resulting creation was going to bestow the taster with magical powers.

'Talking of cocoa pods…' Millie said, her eyes meeting Zach's as he sipped his Red Stripe and cracked open the freshly grilled lobster Lottie had delivered for them to share – it was the freshest seafood she had ever tasted. 'I collected a cocoa pod last night and left it with the others on those wooden crates by the back door intending to dissect it this morning, but they've all disappeared. Did you move them? Or has Claudia got an arrangement with someone to buy them or take them away?'

Millie immediately wished she hadn't brought the subject up. A dark shadow stalked across Zach's expression and his jaw tightened as he clenched his teeth in annoyance.

'No. I didn't move them, and Claudia has not agreed to sell them to anyone either. Why would she when she's worked so hard on improving the cocoa plantation since she and Tim bought it? She cleared the weeds, planted new saplings, even harvested a crop and roasted the beans in the oven behind the garage. Believe me, Claudia and Tim can wax lyrical if you let them about the superior taste of their own product. You should hear them talk about the flavours – "top notes of dry burgundy", "ripe yellow fruits mingled with rich olive oil" – it's as if they're French wine connoisseurs! I don't understand why the pods are disappearing – they're of little value. You're right, it's a mystery, and one I intend to get to the bottom of.'

'Hey! Millie! Good to see you made it. And you've brought Zach with you. Hi, Zach.' Henri offered his palm to Zach and the two men shook hands warmly.

'Actually, I'm not staying. Got a few things to sort out.'

'No problem. Catch you later.'

Millie watched Zach weave his way through the bar and back out to where he had left his quad bike. She had no regrets about having to walk home, but she did wonder why Zach hadn't said goodbye. Clearly, his mind was fixed on something else.

'Hi, Henri. Good to see you. Okay, Millie, here's your very first Andy's Blast. Take it from me – it won't be your last,' declared Lottie, setting a bright blue cocktail down on the table in front of Millie. 'What do you think?'

Millie took a tentative sip and what an explosion of joy on her taste buds! She drained the glass in no time and ordered a second, and then a third, each drink improving in flavour and texture as the afternoon wore on. Henri's friends, Leon and Travis, joined them and the conversation flowed smoothly, covering a range of topics from the serious to the downright ridiculous. Occasionally, Lottie came to sit with them for a drink, as her colleague Marc had materialized by then. Millie only vaguely recalled being guided towards Henri's little red Fiat hours later when the street outside had morphed into an open-air party.

'Guess the Purple Parrot is going to be your local watering hole whilst you're here in Soufrière, eh?'

'Mmm,' murmured Millie, tripping over the kerb and falling into the passenger seat head first, then giggling uncontrollably as Henri drove up the hill to drop her outside her home above the garage.

She waved him off, managed to insert her key into the door and mount the stairs without too much difficulty, and flirted briefly with making a start on the washing-up, but the call of her bed was too strong. She collapsed on the cool cotton sheets and before she knew it she had tumbled into a blissful, dream-free sleep.

Chapter Nine

Millie lingered over her first coffee of the day in an effort to placate the overenthusiastic stonemason hammering away at his masterpiece inside her head. Her tongue felt like sandpaper and for the first time since she'd arrived in St Lucia she wished the Caribbean sun wasn't quite so bright. She had also made a pact with herself that from now on she would always do the washing-up before she went to bed because the sight of the culinary detritus with a storming hangover was enough to make a saint swear. It had taken all her willpower to fill the sink with hot soapy water and return the cooking utensils to their rightful home before allowing herself to indulge in one of the almond croissants that had been mysteriously left on the steps to her studio that morning and was calling her name.

She abandoned her seat on the balcony and stumbled into the bathroom to splash her face with tepid water, taking in her bloodshot eyes and her voluminous hair. She was in the process of brushing her teeth when there was the thunderous roar of an engine followed by a loud hammering on her front door.

'Argh! The kitchen delivery!'

She grabbed her denim shorts and a fresh vest top, dragged her hair into a ponytail and shot downstairs to answer the door.

'Hi,' she breathed.

'Miss Harper?' enquired the delivery guy, his stomach straining against a dirty grey T-shirt and his jeans tucked into heavy, steel-toed work boots. His dreadlocks hung well past his shoulders and his goatee sported three beads in the ubiquitous Caribbean colours of red, green and yellow. The obligatory self-rolled cigarette was attached to his lower lip.

'Erm, yes, yes, but please call me Millie.'

The guy smirked and strode back to the truck, slinging the butt of his cigarette into the trees.

'Just show us where you want this stuff and we'll get to work.'

'Oh, yes, of course.'

Millie's brain throbbed and she struggled to gather her thoughts. She ran back up the stairs to collect the villa's key and almost vomited from the sudden exertion. She bent forward, hands on her knees, taking a moment until her head stopped spinning, but her temples continued to pulsate like the Caribbean beat. She grabbed a glass of water and slung it down her throat before racing to open the back door of the villa.

Somewhere in the dark recesses of her befuddled mind she registered the wooden crates, empty of the cocoa pods, as the delivery guys tossed them out of their way. If anyone had a sensible explanation about their disappearance it would be Ella and she resolved to speak to her about it when she arrived. Was there a thief lurking in the grounds, waiting for the opportunity to steal whatever he could from the plantation? A shiver ran the length of Millie's spine.

'It'll be better if you just let us get on with the unloading, miss,' said the delivery guy with a blatant look that said, Get out of our way.

'Oh, right, of course,' she muttered, backing away through the French doors the men had folded back to ease delivery.

Millie perched guiltily on a sunlounger and watched the trio of men empty the truck of the cardboard boxes that would become the state-of-the-art kitchen from which Claudia would present her Paradise Cookery School courses. As her headache subsided, she made herself useful by preparing a huge jug of fresh lemonade, filled with crushed ice and freshly squeezed lemons and limes. A frisson of pleasure invaded her chest as she watched the men swallow the drink and smack their lips with appreciation. The driver's features softened as he returned his glass to the tray.

'That's some awesome lemonade you make there, miss.'

'Thank you. It's actually a Parisian recipe…'

'Sure it is.'

The men returned to the task of manoeuvring the huge, eight-burner stainless steel stove and industrial-sized fridge-freezer from the veranda into the kitchen, and finally the dishwasher – an absolute necessity.

When the open-plan living area was crammed to the ceiling with cardboard boxes and appliances, the men bade her farewell with smiles and handshakes and disappeared down the hill, accompanied by the ubiquitous thrumming beat of a reggae anthem.

Millie leaned against the balustrade and stared out at the view. She could stay there all day and never tire of the natural beauty of southern St Lucia. She made a promise to herself that if she had any spare time she would ask Henri about arranging a trek up one of the Pitons. She remembered his friend Leon telling her at the Purple Parrot that Gros Piton was the calmer climb of the two and she absolutely had to conquer the hike whilst she was there. And visit the sulphur springs to partake of a mud bath… and take a trip to the drive-in volcano… and the waterfall…

Her eyes began to droop and a wave of tiredness threatened to envelop her. It was already past eight o'clock and there was no sign of the builders despite their assurances via Ella that they would be there when the delivery men arrived. There was nothing she could do until they arrived so she skipped back to her apartment, selected a white string bikini and returned to the pool, slinging her beach bag and towel onto the deckchair before diving into the liquid aquamarine of the infinity pool. The water caressed her senses – just heaven to her aching, journey-bruised limbs and her pounding head. She swam until her mind was clear and her tiredness had been chased into oblivion, before dragging her dripping body to a sunlounger and promptly falling asleep.

'Millie? Millie?'

Millie opened her eyes and a blurry image floated across her vision. For a brief moment, she struggled to remember where she was, why it was so hot, and who had the temerity to wake her from such a glorious dream.

'Mmm?'

'I see the kitchen has been delivered,' said Ella. 'Did you make sure you ticked off every item as it arrived?'

Millie's eyes shot open as she realized with a bolt of panic where she was, and also that she had not thought to check off the items on the inventory. Not the best of starts to her supervisory job. Her skin itched from sunburn and she chastised herself for forgetting to lather on sunscreen. She checked her watch – it was nine o'clock.

'Sorry, Ella, I...'

'Never mind. It looks like we have a more pressing problem to deal with. I see Fitz and his crew haven't arrived yet. They should have been here two hours ago to help with the unloading and to tell the delivery men where to put the boxes.' A splash of annoyance floated across Ella's face but it was swiftly chased away by her broad smile. 'Come on! Let's investigate! It's like Christmas has come again!'

Millie leapt up from the sunbed, excitement swirling through her veins. She stepped into the overcrowded kitchen and promptly stood on the head of a discarded broom whose handle whacked her square on the nose. If she hadn't been fully awake before, she was now.

'Ouch!'

But Ella hadn't noticed her clumsiness. She had already launched herself at one of the huge cardboard boxes, tearing away the tape like a child at a birthday party, before moving on to attack the plastic wrapping surrounding the oven.

'Wow! Just look at this, Millie. It's magnificent. Oh, I can't wait to get started with the cooking.'

'Don't you think we should maybe leave the unpacking until the kitchen fitters arrive?' said Millie, itching to pull off a long strip of cardboard to reveal the front of the fridge in all its stainless-steel glory.

'How can they complain when they should have been here?'

Millie didn't have to be told twice. Together they ripped the protective jacket from the gigantic fridge-freezer, the sinks, the sparkling silver taps, the state-of-the-art coffee machine. Oohs and aahs followed 'Look at this!' and 'Wow!' until they slumped down onto the sunloungers on the veranda completely spent.

Cardboard Chaos reigned.

The kitchen looked as though it had entertained a pack of hyenas on the rampage – sheets of plastic, blankets of bubble wrap, dribbles of polystyrene balls and coils of brown tape scattered the room. Wonky mountains of wooden pallets, cardboard boxes and strips of cornicing reached as high as the ceiling.

Millie giggled. If Zach had been there, he would be rolling his eyes and saying something like, 'Millie? Yes, she can bring chaos to an empty room.' And he was right. She toyed with the idea of taking a photograph on her phone and emailing it to him, but decided not to furnish him with indisputable evidence with which to support his opinion of her. She suspected he would see it for himself soon enough if the tradesmen didn't arrive shortly – they were now over three hours late. It didn't bode well.

With nothing else left to do, Millie made another jug of freshly squeezed lemonade and they relaxed in the shade on the veranda to recover from their exploits and wait for Fitz and his men to arrive.

'So, what will you be doing when you return to the UK, Millie?' asked Ella, rearranging her voluminous emerald-and-saffron skirt around her chubby knees and wiggling her toes out of her sandals.

'Back to my job as a lowly pastry chef in a tiny patisserie in London. Oh, don't get me wrong, it's fun. Étienne is a great boss and he lets me the studio upstairs for a great rent. And I get to work with my best friend Poppy who lives just across the hallway.'

'Have you always lived in London?'

'No, actually, I've only been there for six months. Before that I ran a restaurant in Oxford.' Millie decided not to publicize her Cordon Bleu training. She always felt as though she was boasting when she said it, but she wanted to be truthful with her new friend.

'Did you grow up there? In Oxford?'

'I spent my early childhood in Lourmarin, a village in Provence in the south-east of France. Mum's French, Dad's from Oxford and we moved there when I was seven and my sister was nine. When Dad died two years ago, Mum moved back to France to live with her sister. Jen and I stayed on in Oxford.'

'And is that where you met your friend Poppy?'

'Oh, no, I met Poppy when I started work at Café Étienne.'

'Oh.' Ella turned her head to scrutinize Millie's face. 'I assumed when you said she was your best friend that you had known each other longer.'

How could she explain to kind, sympathetic, wonderful Ella that she had left her life in Oxford behind and that she never wanted to go back? Not even to see her former best friend, Frankie. Of course, Frankie was as mortified about what had happened with Luke as she was, but her loyalties had to lie elsewhere. Millie understood this, but it still hurt tremendously to think about it, so she steered their conversation to the safer ground of her professional life.

'My dream is to be like Claudia and you, Ella. I want to bake, bake, bake until the larder runs dry. I want to craft new recipes from exotic ingredients sourced from all over the world. I want to learn new skills from local chefs and practise until I'm proficient. I want to write cookery books and run my own culinary courses, work in a patisserie in Paris, barbeque steaks in Argentina, advise on pairing spices with fish, meat and seafood. I want to slice vegetables, roast fruit, stir-fry salad.'

'Your mother must be so proud of what you and your sister have achieved.'

'She understands totally how much we both love to work with food. After all, it was her and Gran who inspired us to cook when we were toddlers. She has always urged us to follow our dreams – which is exactly what she is doing now. You should see her on a Saturday night with her friends at the salsa club at the local village hall. And if you saw some of her outfits. Copacabana has nothing on the Glitzy Girls of Lourmarin!'

'Oh, I'd love to meet her. She sounds like my kind of woman.'

Millie smiled at the image of her mother dancing with joyous abandon, squeezing the most out of every moment of her life despite its setbacks. She knew she should strive to emulate her example. After all, her mother had lost her soulmate whilst she and Luke had only been together for a few years. She scooted to the edge of her seat, her arms resting on her knees, staring out over the infinite expanse of the Caribbean Sea, which undulated like a pool of spilled ink beneath a cerulean sky. She fixed her eyes on a brightly coloured bird pecking at a pod on the branch of one of the cocoa trees before skipping off to try something new.

She pulled herself back to reality and resolved to put Luke completely from her mind. St Lucia was a fabulous place to be; not just for its physical beauty, stunning though it was, but for the under-lying current of calm and tranquillity that flowed from the proximity of nature and from its people. Who could complain about doing the dishes when there was that view to distract you from the suds and the wrinkled hands?

'They're here!' declared Ella, pushing herself up from the sunlounger.

Accompanied by a fanfare of reggae music, a white van screeched to a halt in the courtyard and three men tumbled from the front seat.

Millie glanced at her watch. Ten-thirty. Not a good start. She cast a worried look at Ella who nodded her agreement. They would have to express their concern about timekeeping from the outset otherwise the project would never be completed in time for the wedding guests. They needed the guys to turn up on the dot of seven a.m. every day in order to achieve the deadline, which meant they were already behind before they had even started. Anxiety gnawed at the pit of Millie's stomach.

'This it?' asked the boss as he chewed on his unlit cigarette, his brown eyes widened in surprise. 'Was the kitchen delivered like this?'

'There's no point in taking the offensive, Fitzgerald Clarke. You're over three hours late and it just won't do. I intend to have a word with your mother about your timekeeping unless you stay late to make up for what's been lost today. You are fully aware how tight the schedule is. I shall expect you to stick to your promise to have everything finished by next Friday. This is Amelia Harper who will be overseeing the project. Don't think of messing her around or you'll have me to answer to.'

Fitz and his two friends stared at the diminutive chef, their lips curled into smiles of amused contrition, but Millie could see a soupçon of apprehension in their eyes. Ella pushed her way past them and through the jungle of cardboard to retrieve the plans.

'Now, these are the specifications. It all looks pretty straightforward. What are you waiting for?'

Millie loved the way Ella's Caribbean accent became much more pronounced when she spoke to her fellow St Lucians. She watched as Fitz opened his mouth and closed it again on seeing the steely determination in Ella's expression. He removed the cigarette from his lips, shoved it in the pocket of his low-slung jeans and swept his dreadlocks from his lined face.

'No worries, Ella. Me and my men will make sure that you have the best kitchen in the whole of St Lucia.' Fitz offered Millie his hand before turning to his workmates. 'Pleased to meet you, Amelia. This is Alphonse, but we call him Alph, and this is Vic.'

'Oh, please, call me Millie.'

The two young men in dusty jeans and ancient Bob Marley T-shirts offered Ella a respectful nod and a quick smile of acknowledgement to Millie but didn't venture any conversation.

'Ah, Alph, yes, I thought I recognized you. I know your Aunt Effie. She's treasurer of our village council.' Ella's mahogany eyes held Alph's for several seconds and Millie thought she saw him cower. All three men had clearly got the message that their tardiness would not be tolerated from here on in. Ella Johnson was not a woman to be messed with.

'Yes, Ms Johnson. No worries. Sorry we're late today but…' He glanced at Fitz for support but he had wisely disappeared into the kitchen with Vic and started to remove the plastic wrapping from the huge slabs of marble that would one day soon become the bench tops for the very first Paradise Cookery School.

Millie couldn't help smiling. It was obvious they had hoped this would be an easy, laid-back job in a beautiful villa overlooking spectacular scenery with an infinity pool to cool off in after a hard day's toil. They hadn't factored in the indomitable Ella Johnson being on site to crack the whip and oversee their timekeeping. She experienced a surge of gratefulness for Claudia's friend's presence, acknowledging her own weakness for succumbing to a well-argued excuse. The Paradise Cookery School would never be delivered on time if it was solely down to her.

'Now, Millie and I have important work to do organizing the menus, making shopping lists and testing out the recipes. If you need anything we will be in the kitchen in the studio above the garage over there. There's a lot for us all to do and we'll stay out of your way provided you press on with the work. Friday the sixteenth is the deadline. That'll leave Millie and I only two days to make sure the place is spotless and to stock the cupboards for the arrival of our first students. Don't forget, Fitz, time seeps through our fingers no matter how hard we try to snatch it back. The kitchen must be ready on schedule. I expect to see you here at seven o'clock sharp tomorrow morning.'

'Yes. Yes, ma'am. So, seven a.m. on the dot it is!'

Fitz gestured to Alph and Vic whose jaws had dropped as they listened to Ella's orders. The three amigos nodded in unison and attacked the renovations with a vengeance to the sound track of Eddie Grant throbbing from the speakers of a paint-splattered stereo.

'Thanks, Ella. I don't think the men would have listened to me. I suspect that you've just saved the whole project from certain failure. I owe you.'

'Lovely,' smiled Ella, bustling up the stairs to Millie's tiny kitchen. 'You can repay me immediately by showing me how to make chocolate millefeuille and pistachio macaroons and a perfect *beurre blanc*!'

'Only if you show me how to cook authentic Creole dishes with local spices.'

Millie smiled at Ella's enthusiasm to experiment with French recipes. Her culinary zeal reminded Millie of her own passion for all things gastronomic before the fiasco with Luke had wiped all the joy from her soul. However, she was rediscovering her culinary hunger. Ella's desire to learn something new was infectious and she felt her spirits nudge northwards. It felt good to be asked to pass on her knowledge and skills and she was keen to get started.

A companionable silence descended as they sifted flour and whisked eggs and an idea began to snake its way round Millie's brain – the birth of a dream that she had never thought possible before that day. Maybe, one day in the not-too-distant future, Claudia would allow her to present a course on French cooking to a class at the Paradise Cookery School. How fabulous would that be, doing what she loved most in the world against such an idyllic backdrop?

The only seed of doubt in her mind was whether she could come to terms with what had happened with Luke in Oxford and fly away from the wreckage of their relationship. For the first time since the bombshell had landed, she truly thought she could. What was the alternative? Instead of starring in the lead role of her life, choosing to consign herself to that of supporting actress as a spinster aunt to Jen's two daughters, Lily and Odette? There was no way she intended to die alone surrounded by a glut of uneaten macaroons!

It was time to move on.

Chapter Ten

The next morning Millie awoke to a clear head and the birds rehearsing their daily symphony instead of the usual cacophony of slamming doors and thundering traffic outside her tiny studio apartment above Café Étienne. Not only that, the views from their respective windows occupied diametrically opposed ends of the visual spectrum.

Here in St Lucia, the Pitons wore nature's cloak of dappled sunlight, their lush flanks shimmering in the breeze like an emerald waterfall. At home, her view over the rain-soaked rooftops rewarded her with a forest of redundant chimney pots, twisted TV aerials and satellite dishes. London did many things superbly, but one thing St Lucia topped the index in was its laid-back lifestyle. There was no frantic commute to the office, bistro or patisserie to work harder, faster and longer until your brain was frazzled and your dreams extinguished.

As she sipped her cappuccino, sprinkled with a dash of locally cultivated nutmeg, her reverie injected a surprise pang of homesickness into her stomach. She thought of Jen, getting Lily and Odette ready for school before dashing off to present a cookery demonstration at the WI or the local college or village fair. She couldn't wait to share what she had learned so far about the intricacies of the indigenous flavours of the Caribbean with her sister.

She thought of Poppy, dressing for her shift at the patisserie, cursing as she shot down the four flights of stairs from her flat, late as usual. Luckily, Poppy was a prolific emailer and had kept her up to date with all the gossip at Café Étienne. This morning's missive was all about a potential date with a guy from the Italian deli across the road. Millie had wished her luck and demanded a photograph, attaching her own of Zach and Henri in return. She had just read her friend's reply but could have predicted her comments and her preference. Poppy adored men like Henri; intelligent, community-focused, clean-shaven with a strong jaw, neatly clipped hair, French Caribbean heritage – ideal boyfriend material in fact, save for the lengthy commute for dinner.

She tossed her coffee cup into the sink and helped herself to a plate of chopped tropical fruit from the fridge – mango, pineapple, melon, guava

– then went out to the balcony to continue her contemplations.

It was not yet seven a.m. and already the sun was poking its face over the horizon, casting rippling fissures of pale amber and scarlet over the sea. It was beautiful and she would never grow tired of sitting on the rattan chair staring at the ever-changing panorama. At that time in the morning the air was cooler and the humidity lower – it was the best time to enjoy the peace and tranquillity, as well as the sweet aroma of jasmine floating on the gentle breeze.

She selected a slice of pineapple and allowed its sweetness to trickle slowly from her tongue down her throat – pure liquid paradise. She finished her breakfast and grabbed a quick shower before pulling on her white capri pants and strappy scarlet T-shirt, gathering her straw-like hair into a high ponytail and trotting down the stairs to check on Fitz's progress.

By the time she arrived on the veranda, the sun had joined the day and bathed the whole scene in a golden glow, but there was no sign of Fitz. She glanced at her watch to see it was seven-forty-five – so much for Ella's lecture on timekeeping. She sighed. If Ella couldn't impress upon the men to be on time, she had no additional ammunition in her own armoury.

Millie planned to spend the day as she had yesterday; triple-testing the recipes that would form the course's itinerary. If she concentrated on two dishes each day – sourcing the ingredients, preparing the recipes, taste-testing and gauging the preparation and cooking time – then she would be finished by next Friday.

Claudia was relying on her judgement and she had asked for a daily email with her findings and recommendations. She had explained to Millie that the Paradise Cookery School courses were to be intensive week-long programmes with a variety of themes, some of which could be tailor-made to the guests' personal preferences, like the Chocolate & Confetti one arranged for the following week. Once the hotel side of things was up and running, Claudia was also planning to offer a more general course focusing on the preparation of a Caribbean-inspired starter, main meal and dessert each day. The resulting culinary masterpieces would then be consumed at a communal dinner each evening with local wine and spirits or home-made fruit punch. Each guest would be asked to score their fellow chefs out of ten, with accomplishment certificates available for those requiring them. Claudia hoped the students would take the school seriously, but Millie knew that a handful of them would be attending for the social aspects of meeting like-minded people, maybe even hoping to hook up with a potential date. Or indulge in a holiday fling just as Jen had suggested she should!

She decided to grab the bull by the horns and ring Fitz. Instead of leaving the villa via the French doors she opened the back door, stooping forward to remove one of the wooden crates that was blocking her access to the courtyard. It was heavier than she had expected. She dislodged the lid and to her surprise she saw the crate was filled with the purple-brown cocoa pods wrapped in a fresh crop of banana leaves.

Oh, God! Could she have missed them the previous day? No way, she wasn't crazy! The boxes had definitely both been empty. She screwed up her eyes and shook her head, but she was not mistaken or hallucinating. Someone had replenished the crates.

The piercing shriek of an engine straining to ascend the incline interrupted the internal cross-examination of her sanity.

'Hey, Millie! Good morning!' sang Fitz in his infectious Caribbean lilt as he leapt from the cab of his rust-blistered white van, gifting her with a broad smile. That morning he had moved up in the world by ditching the self-rolled cigarette for a thick, Caribbean cigar.

Alph and Vic shouted a friendly greeting, strolled to the back of the vehicle and prised open the double doors. Flakes of rust dribbled from the lock and hinges like dried blood. Vic extracted the largest stereo radio Millie had ever seen, liberally doused in lumps of plaster and splashes of paint, and carried it on his shoulder to the veranda at the front of the villa.

Millie resisted the temptation to check her watch but she knew it was well past eight o'clock. She forced a smile on her lips and followed the trio to the veranda where they deposited their canvas tool bags before carrying their lunch pails into the kitchen.

'Man, you can never get tired of this view, eh?' said Fitz, his hands on his hips, stretching out his back muscles as though he had just rolled out of bed. He probably had, thought Millie with a jolt of annoyance.

'True. I'll get the coffee brewing, shall I?'

Millie made a swift getaway as she suspected Fitz was about to launch into an unprovoked monologue on the myriad benefits of St Lucia over London, Paris and that twenty-four-hour metropolis, New York. It was his favourite special-ized subject and she had heard the lecture twice already. She refused to give them any reason to delay their day any further. All three men possessed that laid-back vibe, which they had clearly honed to perfection over the years, and nothing and no one could hurry them along. She wished she could bottle just a smidgeon of that stress-free lifestyle and smuggle it back to London where most of the time she felt frazzled and exhausted. She prayed that, despite their attitude to timekeeping, their workmanship would be up to scratch.

She tossed a handful of coffee beans into the grinder and set a cafetière and three sturdy mugs on a tray. She didn't have to be a clairvoyant to predict that these items of crockery would be well used over the next two weeks. Carrying the tray from her studio across to the villa, she found the men congregated round a cardboard box, scoffing thick jerk-chicken sandwiches and chuckling about the exploits of someone called Jacques like a trio of fishwives.

She set the tray down and gave the gang what she hoped was a meaningful stare. 'Claudia really needs the kitchen to be ready for her inspection on the sixteenth. There seems a lot to do so I'll let you get started.'

'Chill, man. We are craftsmen, artisans. You can't hurry perfection. Did Leonardo da Vinci rush to finish the *Mona Lisa*? Did Michelangelo rush to finish the Sistine Chapel? No. They were allowed to take their time to express their creativity. Don't worry, Millie. Be happy!'

'Right, well, I agree that creativity is important and Claudia *is* keen that everything in the kitchen is finished to an ultra-high standard. But equally as important is delivering on time, because if she has to cancel the Chocolate & Confetti classes, the Paradise Cookery School might never get off the ground. I don't think Ella will be very happy if her dream to become a cookery-school demonstrator is dashed because the sinks aren't fitted, do you?'

Millie's heart hammered painfully against her ribcage and her cheeks had flooded with colour, but she felt a surge of elation at the assertiveness she had displayed. She left the kitchen and strode down to the pool, inhaling deep, rejuvenating breaths when she knew she was out of sight of the men.

The sun had climbed mercilessly in the clear azure sky, sending the temperature on a steep uphill trajectory. Even in the shade of the leafy canopy around the pool terrace, the air was thick and oppressive. The humidity pressed into Millie's chest, robbing her of a clear draw of breath, until relief flooded her veins when the rhythmic beat of calypso was accompanied by the sound of a hammer and circular saw.

Millie made a decision. It was time to take a closer look at the cocoa pods which, if Claudia had her way, would form part of the ethos and branding for the Paradise Cookery School. She selected a couple from the top crate and carried them towards her studio like precious cargo.

'Hey, where do you think you're tiptoeing off to with those?'

Millie experienced a flash of guilt before meeting Zach's accusatory stare.

'Oh, I didn't think anyone would mind. I didn't take them from the trees. I found them in the crates over there. Did you pack them?'

'No, I didn't.'

Millie saw a look of annoyance stalk across Zach's expression and she opened her mouth to offer to return them, but Zach spoke first.

'Fancy an excursion?'

'What sort of excursion?'

She had a vision of them bucking and diving across the rough terrain on the back of the quad bike before indulging in a session of wild swimming in one of the mountain streams and cooking their dinner on a campfire. Maybe they would have to forage for edible bugs! Eeuw! And anyway, shouldn't she be staying at the villa to oversee the workmen's progress?

'I'm not sure about leaving Fitz and his crew to their own devices…'

'All sorted. I've spoken to Ella and she's happy to hold the fort for a while.'

Zach had followed her up the stairs to her studio. Although the kitchen was an improvement on the previous day's explosion of culinary chaos, it still bore the scars of that morning's breakfast. Zach was staring with abject disgust at the pile of crockery shoved higgledy-piggledy in the sink. Before he could launch into a litany of criticism on her housekeeping skills, she decided to accept his offer.

'An excursion sounds great, then. What did you have in mind?'

'How does a personalized orientation tour sound? I was thinking maybe the Botanical Gardens, the Sulphur Springs, the Diamond Falls? Come on, let's get out of here. I don't know how you do it, but this kitchen looks like Downtown Fallujah. Claudia usually keeps everything pristine and organized, you know.'

Millie ignored his criticism, grabbed her purse and swapped her sandals for a pair of embroidered crimson Sketchers. She was keen to visit the famous multicoloured Diamond Waterfalls and she didn't think sequinned flip-flops were the ideal footwear.

'So, your chariot awaits, Princess Pretty Shoes.'

Zach gave a theatrical bow, his dark features more akin to the villain of the show than to Prince Charming. But when Millie saw what he was pointing to, her heart sang. Her 'chariot' was a lipstick-red BMW Roadster Convertible.

'Wow! Is this yours?'

Zach laughed. 'No. It's Tim's, but he doesn't mind if I use it when he's over in the UK.'

Millie smiled. This was exactly the sort of excursion she could get used to.

Chapter Eleven

They drove down the hill towards Soufrière. Some of the houses on the outskirts of the town were little more than sheds with corrugated-iron rooftops, but they had been proudly painted with bright Caribbean hues of emerald, aquamarine and sunflower yellow. She wondered how such flimsy structures managed to withstand the daily dose of what Clavie had labelled liquid sunshine, never mind the not-infrequent hurricanes.

They reached the harbour and Millie skimmed her eyes over the storefronts, which were awash with exuberantly coloured souvenirs, busy with bustling tourists from the two yachts moored at the jetty. Young boys swam in the sea at the boats' sterns, squealing to those on board to throw in coins for them to retrieve from the seabed.

Millie couldn't help but smile as they passed the Purple Parrot and saw Andrew in the alleyway indulging in a forbidden cigarette, his bandana – today's blue – knotted around his neck.

They passed Dylan's Dive Shack around which a disparate collection of surfboards and kayaks were scattered, along with rails of wetsuits drying in the sun. Dylan himself lounged in a white plastic chair, his ankle over his knee, plugged into his iPod, tapping his foot to the beat. She cast her eyes over her shoulder to the wooden veranda of the Purple Parrot and was not in the least bit surprised to see Lottie loitering on the steps as she delivered a tray of lunchtime drinks to thirsty patrons, her eyes resting on the object of her affection, her burgundy hair streaming in the breeze.

'Doesn't Dylan realize Lottie adores him?'

'You've noticed that too?'

'How can you not!' she laughed.

Zach swung the steering wheel to the right, taking the road that skirted the foothills of the Pitons. They left the streets of Soufrière behind and followed the signs for the Diamond Falls Botanical Gardens.

'I don't think Dylan realizes the extent of her devotion. He's happy with his life as it is. He has his business; he works with his best friend, Ryan, and the third musketeer in his group, Elijah, works up at one of the luxury five-star resorts in the next bay. And there's Marc, of course, who works at the Purple Parrot with Lottie.'

'Sounds like an idyllic life.'

'Dylan tumbles into a romance every other week with a girl who's desperate for a holiday fling to boast about when she returns home to the wind and rain. You could write an epic novel about his exploits. Who better to cavort with for a while than a golden-tanned surfer dude with his own diving school? Alone in the boat, drifting serenely under a perfect sky, reliant on each other for your safety as you swim beneath the sapphire waves exploring the magnificent coral and all those secluded coves. Dylan's been here for ten years and I don't think he has plans to leave any time soon. Hang on!'

Zach swung the Roadster into a hidden clearing and jumped out.

'Here's the path. Come on, slowcoach! Watch out for the snakes!'

Zach forged ahead through the dense vegetation, occasionally slapping away an errant branch as Millie trotted in his wake. The intense heat prickled at the back of her neck and beneath her breasts as she tuned in to the gentle symphony that accompanied their walk through the rainforest – the call of the doves, hawks and St Lucian orioles mingled with the cicadas, frogs and trickling water.

They trekked in silence for a while, appreciating the splendour of nature's diversity. Millie could tell that Zach was happier in these surroundings, mellower, more relaxed. Occasionally, he paused to point out a particular plant or flower, shrub or tree.

'This one is a White Cedar and this is Mahogany. But can you guess what this is?'

'No idea.'

'This tree produces the mace and the nutmeg you probably use every day in your baking. The mace is the lacy golden-brown wrapping which is removed and dried, and the nutmeg is the seed kernel inside.'

Millie fingered the hard, outer shell of the nutmeg, pulling a branch down to her nostrils and sniffing, but, of course, it didn't emit the familiar aroma. Every recipe she made requiring a sprinkle of grated nutmeg would now take on a whole new meaning.

When they rounded the next bend in the path, Millie's jaw dropped. They had arrived at the Diamond Falls where the river tumbled through the sunshine, over a rocky outcrop, producing a kaleidoscope of colours into a pool below.

'Wow!'

'Gorgeous, isn't it?'

'What makes the waterfall so colourful?'

Millie walked to the edge of the falls as a group of chattering French tourists dutifully followed their tour guide back along a wide pathway to the car park. She reached for her phone and began clicking photographs to send to Jen and Poppy.

'The stream is laced with volcanic minerals: sulphur, copper sulphate, magnesium, iron, manganese and calcium from the Pitons. Come on. This way!'

Zach branched out in the opposite direction to the tourists along a deserted footpath. After half an hour or so of pleasant, picturesque strolling, the gradient increased sharply and Millie's calf muscles screamed at the unfamiliar exertion.

'Hey, Zach, can we stop for a minute?' she pleaded, her breath coming in spurts, sweat trickling down between her shoulder blades.

'It's just a little further. I promise you it'll be worth it.'

Another ten minutes' hard climb and they rounded the corner of a leaf-strewn pathway. As Millie rested her palms on her knees, drawing in gulps of thick balmy oxygen, she raised her head and gaped. The view spread before her was so majestic that her emotions got the better of her and tears pricked at the corners of her eyes.

They were almost halfway up Gros Piton, with the rich sapphire of the Caribbean Sea sparkling to their left, the glossy rainforest to their right, and nestled in the groove in between were the terracotta roofs of Soufrière. The lush vegetation encircled the urban development below like a laurel wreath surrounding a rose-coloured jewel. Fishing boats, sleek white yachts, ferries and old-fashioned clippers dotted the ocean.

A gasp escaped her lips. 'It's just so…'

A plethora of words tumbled around in her head but she discarded each one as inadequate. Her lexicon of admiration had been erased from her memory by the overwhelming beauty in front of her. They stood in appreciative silence for a long time, sipping from a water bottle, until Millie was jolted from her trance by a large bullet of water slapping onto the back of the hand shading her eyes from the sun.

'Oh, no! It's almost three o'clock!' she gasped, ducking her head and shoulders as the habitual bombardment of rain increased in velocity.

'Come on.'

Zach grabbed her hand and together they lurched, tripped and skidded down a hidden trail until the deluge prevented further advancement. Once again, Millie experienced the questionable pleasure of being drenched through to her under-wear. She dragged her hair from her face and flicked it behind her ears. The pungent scent of rotting vegetation caused her throat to constrict and her skin to break out in a ripple of goose pimples. She stood in front of Zach, her arms by her sides, raindrops dripping from her nose. Laughing, he said, 'Just another fifty yards, I promise.'

He hooked his arm around her waist and, true to his word, within a few moments they had arrived at a tiny wooden hut huddled beneath a canopy of palm trees, with a tattered veranda and a front door painted in sunshine yellow. Zach dislodged one of the terracotta pots crammed with pink orchids to reveal a large silver key. He slotted it into the lock and they tumbled in out of the rain.

'What is this place?'

'It's a ranger's cabin. A friend of mine, Mathias, works for the Botanical Gardens. He uses it to shelter from the rain and, on occasion for... well, you know.'

Millie glanced round the one-room shelter. Yes, it was definitely an ideal love nest – two plump leather sofas draped with mohair throws, a woven scatter rug and a pair of intricately carved masks decorating the walls. She giggled as she wondered if the wooden artefacts were some kind of fertility symbols.

She raised her eyes to Zach, intending to mention the artwork, but when she saw the expression on his face her breath caught in her throat. Heat rushed through her body and the shivers rippling up and down her spine had nothing to do with the drop in temperature inside the cabin. Her heart bounced to her toes and back into her ribcage as her brain tried to dissect the reason for her surprise reaction.

Zach took a step towards her, holding her eyes, his lips parted slightly. A blast of goose-pimples washed over her forearms and sent blood rushing to her cheeks and thrumming through her ears. When his hand touched hers, it took a supreme effort not to flinch from the spark of electricity that shot through her veins and southwards.

'You're trembling.'

'I...'

Millie found that she couldn't formulate a coherent sentence. She felt as though her brain had been temporarily disconnected from its modem. It was almost a relief when Zach severed their connection to grab a couple of fluffy white towels from a cupboard in the corner. He tossed one over to her and she took her time drying her arms and legs, then towelling her hair to allow her thoughts to calm and the colour in her cheeks to fade.

What just happened? screamed her brain when at last it caught up with her body's swirling emotions.

She flopped down on one of the sofas and peered at Zach from beneath her lashes. He had his back to her, fiddling with a box of matches and a storm lantern. She took a moment to enjoy the way his wet T-shirt clung to his broad, muscular shoulders and the tufts of ebony hair sprang from his crown. With the towel draped around his neck he looked like a boxer in the ring, and when her eyes followed the contours of his body downwards a blast of desire detonated in her lower abdomen. She swiftly averted her gaze, but not before Zach had spun round and caught her ogling his buttocks.

'Here.' He handed her a bottle of water and smirked.

Just as she always did when she was embarrassed or thrust unexpectedly into an awkward situation, Millie couldn't help herself from launching into a garbled monologue of inconsequential utterings as she fidgeted with the tassels on the mohair throw.

'Thank you for showing me the waterfall, Zach. It was amazing! I love St Lucia. You are so lucky to be able to call it your home, even if it is temporarily.

I can completely understand why Dylan and Lottie don't want to leave and Andrew started a business here. I absolutely adore the fact that the sun shines every day, that there's an abundance of fresh produce all year round. I love the Creole cuisine, the calypso music, the friendliness of the people. I could even get used to the rain, especially as it only seems to last thirty minutes before reverting to luscious sunshine again. Oh, look! I think it's stopped!'

She leapt from her seat and dashed to the door, wrenching it open to peer outside. It hadn't.

'Can't have a tropical rainforest without the rain,' Zach mused, calmly crossing his ankle over his knee and stretching his arms behind his head, ignoring her strange behaviour.

The daily downpour continued to hammer its staccato tune on the tiled roof overhead, but instead of feeling safe and dry inside the little hut, Millie felt claustrophobic. Something had changed between her and Zach, and whilst she much preferred the Zach she had spent time with that day to the snippy, sarcastic one she had first met, she still felt unsettled at the pull of attraction she had experienced. She craved some time to herself to analyse exactly what it meant, but she would have to wait. Instead, she decided to raise something that had been bothering her all day.

'Zach?'

'Mmm?'

'You remember we were talking about the mysterious disappearance of the cocoa pods when we were at the Purple Parrot a couple of days ago?'

'Yes.'

'I know this is going to sound weird, but did you refill those empty crates at the back door of the villa?'

Zach sat upright and stared at her.

'No. Why?'

'Because when I checked them this morning they were full again. Are you sure Claudia doesn't have an arrangement to sell them to someone?'

'I'm absolutely sure. If she did, I would know about it. There's no point in trying to sell them. They have to be harvested on a commercial scale to be viable and at the moment Claudia's just dabbling, a hobby really because of her interest in food.'

'Does anyone else nearby grow cocoa?'

'There *is* a fully renovated plantation in the Soufrière hills that grows the crop commercially. They ship it back to their factories in the UK to make their own luxury brand of chocolate. They even offer holidays and tours of the plantation so that guests can see the process of chocolate-making first-hand and then indulge in tasting the finished product. Theirs is a huge enterprise – Claudia's plantation is only a couple of acres.'

'Mm, that's what I thought. It's strange, that's all.'

'Don't worry about it,' said Zach, his tone telling her that was the end of her line of enquiry and to change the subject. She wondered why, but a moment later her curiosity vanished as Zach ventured into much more uncomfortable territory. 'So, doesn't your boyfriend mind you spending a whole two weeks in the Caribbean without him?'

Indecision floated through Millie's mind as she wondered whether she could open up her heart, even a smidgeon, to this prickly man, despite their recent rapprochement. She wished there was something a little stronger than bottled water in the hut to give her the strength to deliver the sad synopsis of her life. An Andy's Blast cocktail would have done nicely – alcohol had become a supportive friend over the last six months and she had regularly found solace in the arms of Ricard and Martell and Gordon.

A feeling of total panic swirled around her body. She waited until her heartbeat calmed from sprint to walking pace and inhaled a deep, steadying breath. Zach was watching her as she wrestled with her demons but had wisely decided to remain silent.

'I don't have a boyfriend,' she began, but she just couldn't go any further. Her throat was obstructed by a stone the size of a coconut and she felt as though there was a block of concrete squeezing all the air out of her lungs. To cover her distress, she decided to spin the conversation round to Zach. There must be a reason why he had ended up single-handedly running a dilapidated cocoa planation in the tropical rainforest of St Lucia. 'What about you? How are you finding life running a cocoa plantation?'

Zach gave her one of his familiar eye rolls. He clearly knew an avoidance tactic when he saw one, but he let it pass.

'Well, it's a bit different to working in the Cotswolds, that's for sure. But when Jake's mother was taken into hospital, he wanted to spend some time back in the UK and asked if I wanted to do a swap for six months. Who could refuse?'

'But you couldn't have been a cocoa grower in the Cotswolds,' she blurted out before thinking her words through, her fuzzy, anxiety-ridden mind beginning to throb with the rising humidity.

'I'm not a bloody gardener! I'm an estate manager! I have an honours degree in business management and I also have an internationally recognized qualification in horticulture. Tree disease is a constant threat wherever you are in the world. Here in St Lucia, its spread has a devastating environmental impact not only on the rainforest but on the various species it supports. Without constant expert care Claudia and Tim's fledgling crop of cocoa palms will be decimated.'

'Sorry, I didn't mean to insult your work.'

'Oh, don't worry about offending me,' Zach laughed, relieving the tension that had been building in the tiny wooden room. Dimples appeared around his lips like cute brackets and Millie could see the return of the habitual sarcastic gleam in his mahogany eyes. 'After all, I'm British. I'll just tuck your comments away in a crevice of my brain to fester for a while before dissecting their meaning repeatedly until my self-esteem plunges to the bottom of the barrel.'

And there he is, she thought, back to the old Zach, tossing grenades along the conversational path.

It was her turn to remain silent as Zach weighed up whether to share a little more of his personal story with her. He leaned forward and placed his bottle of water carefully onto a beer mat before sitting back into the folds of the sofa. Unlike her, he had no qualms about seeking out her eyes.

'Everyone has heartaches to deal with at some point in their lives, either their own or from standing on the sidelines of loved ones when they are hurting. Whenever I think of my parents' divorce I still get a jab of surprise that they're no longer together. But they're both doing fine. In fact, I would even hazard a guess that Mum is happier now than she was with Dad over the last few years. She left London and went back to Berryford where she grew up and is surrounded by the same close-knit community of her childhood and a coterie of renewed and new acquaintances. Yes, she has definitely moved on.

'But in order to do that successfully we all need to look at the man, or woman, in the mirror. Why did I take the job at the plantation? Well, I took it for several reasons; the main one being to escape from the pressure my ex-girlfriend was applying to our relationship for the purchase of an engagement ring. Chloe and I had only been dating for six months and we *were* chugging along nicely. But, marriage? I knew that wasn't on the cards and it was only fair to have the "It's not you, it's me" conversation straight away.

'Chloe was devastated, and things got emotional for a few weeks. I promised she could have as long as she needed to find a new place to live. So, when Tim told me he was looking for someone to cover for Jake over here in St Lucia, I jumped at the chance to ditch the reproachful stares and uncomfortable silences and escape. Mind you, it didn't take Chloe long to move on. She's just splashed photographs of an over-the-top diamond solitaire all over her Facebook page, accompanied by a ream of selfies of herself and a guy called Mario at the top of the Eiffel Tower where he's apparently just proposed. I couldn't be happier for her.'

Millie scrutinized his tanned face for a wrinkle of regret, but there wasn't one. In that moment, she wished she could swap places with him as it seemed his story was a mirror image of her own. She knew exactly how Chloe must have felt, although she and Luke had been together for a lot longer and if she believed Zach's version of events, no one else had been involved in their break-up. But she took huge encouragement from the fact that his ex-girlfriend had found love again and had the ring to prove it.

Her spirits ratcheted up another notch. She was amazed at the steps forward she had taken since arriving in the Caribbean. All she had to do now was dip her toe in the water of the dating game and she could label herself as cured of the melancholy and hurt that had descended on the day Luke had made his surprise announcement. However, despite the emotional progress she had made, she still wasn't ready to share the details with anyone, even Zach who had just bared his heart to her.

'Come on. The rain's stopped now. Fancy a drink at the Purple Parrot on the way back? Or are you champing at the bit to see what Fitz and his men have been doing today?'

'Well, yes, I am, but I also feel guilty about leaving Ella to do all the recipe testing today while I indulge in an undeserved day off trekking through a tropical paradise.'

'I told you, Ella was more than happy to spend the day whipping up a plethora of Caribbean culinary masterpieces. In fact, it was her idea that we rounded off our day sightseeing with a customary drink at her favourite bar.'

'Okay, since you put it like that, a drink would be great, thanks.'

She pushed herself to her feet too quickly. Her straw bag toppled from her shoulder, spilling its contents onto the floor at her feet.

'I wish you could blame your constant clumsiness on the potent Caribbean rum, but we haven't had any!'

When Millie had collected her belongings, they made their way back to where Zach had left the Roadster, the rain-soaked vegetation slashing at their knees and shins and sprinkling a shower of raindrops onto their shoulders. The air was still rich with humidity and the fragrance of damp soil hit the back of her throat. A silken veil of vapour lingered between the ferns on either side of the pathway as the birds resumed their afternoon sonata in the canopy overhead. To Millie, it was as close to her idea of the Garden of Eden as it was possible to get and she was glad she had shared the experience with Zach.

'I've really enjoyed our excursion. Thanks for bringing me here.'

'Next time it's the Sulphur Springs and mud baths. You can be as messy and clumsy as you like there. Just don't forget to bring your costume!'

Chapter Twelve

They pulled into a parking space outside the Purple Parrot. It was four-thirty and only a smattering of the customers were still loitering over their rum cocktail or Red Stripe before returning to the beach for their final dose of sunshine. Zach grabbed his usual table at the corner of the veranda and whilst they waited for Lottie to take their order, they watched Dylan and Ryan drag their boat into the shallows and help two giggling girls to step down from the deck.

'Hi, Lottie. Two Red Stripes, please.'

'Oh, could I have a lemonade instead?' asked Millie, keen to keep a clear head. She would need to inspect the workmen's progress when she got back.

'Coming right up.'

A couple of minutes later, Lottie set down their drinks on the scarred table and joined them, dejection scrawled across her pretty features, her eyes lowered as she picked the label from her beer bottle.

Then, when it was completely torn away, she fiddled with the brightly coloured string bracelets around her wrists, her shoulders curved in to her chest. Not the go-to demeanour Millie expected of a young girl who had chosen to stay on after her gap year in an idyllic paradise.

'Is everything okay, Lottie?' Zach asked, catching Millie's eye and raising his eyebrows when Lottie slammed her elbows onto the table like a petulant toddler, cupping her chin in her palms.

'No. Actually, I'm thinking of going home.'

'What? To Anisha's?'

'Not to Anisha's,' she snapped, thumping her beer bottle on the table, casting her hundredth glance in the direction of Dylan's Dive Shack where Dylan and Ryan were still laughing and jostling with the two young holidaymakers.

'Ah,' said Zach, understanding immediately.

Lottie flashed him a scowl, challenging him to vocalize her distress, but Zach wasn't stupid enough to attempt to charter those turbulent waters. He, and everyone else at the Purple Parrot who cared to study Lottie's behaviour, knew the only reason Lottie had stayed on in St Lucia was Dylan. She had learned to dive, learned to sail the *Nigella*, and joined him and Ryan – whenever her shifts allowed

– at beach parties, barbeques and charity events. She followed him everywhere.

Lottie let out a ragged sigh. 'I've spoken to Andy. I'm going back to Cardiff. I told him there's no point in me sticking around here. I'm obviously wasting my time.'

'What did Andy say?' asked Zach.

'What do you think he said? It's one of his busiest times. Obviously he can't rely on Marc – he's useless. He's never on time, always messes up the orders and he doesn't just flirt with the customers, if you get my drift. The restaurant is struggling, too.'

'What do you mean?'

'Well, you know…' Lottie twisted in her seat, staring at the empty bottle in her hand as if wondering where its contents had disappeared to. 'With the recession and everything. Takings are down, expenses are up. I told Andy that he should dock Marc's wages every time he's late, but he doesn't want to lose him.'

Lottie rolled her eyes. Millie marvelled at the fact that Dylan could possibly have failed to notice her beauty. Fresh, youthful skin tinted to a pale honey hue, a smattering of freckles across the bridge of her nose and the cutest chin.

'How's Anisha?' asked Zach. 'What will she do with the studio if you leave?'

'I don't know, but things are the same at her shop. Takings are down. Tourists are still buying her sarongs and bikinis, but the local souvenirs aren't shifting. Even sales of Travis's gorgeous artwork and carvings have been slow this year. And, for what it's worth, Anisha agrees with me. Men are just not worth the effort.'

'No progress with Leon then?'

'No. I've told her she should move on too.' Lottie turned to Millie. 'Do you have someone special back home?'

'No, there's no one special. I've just come out of a long-term relationship, so no dates since... well, since April.'

Lottie's face brightened as she scooted to the edge of her rattan chair and shot a mischievous look at Zach. Millie sent up a swift prayer to her guardian angel that Lottie wasn't about to suggest Zach. She would have died of embarrassment. 'Well, we'll just have to put an end to that run of luck, won't we?'

'Hang on, Lottie, I...'

'Just a date. I'm not suggesting you rush off and get engaged.'

Clearly Lottie's earlier despondency about all things love- and romance-related had floated from her mind on the wings of Cupid. Millie looked across to Zach for his support but he simply shrugged and leaned back in his chair ready to enjoy the show.

'No, thanks, Lottie. I'm only over here to supervise the kitchen renovations for the Paradise Cookery School. And Ella and I will be spending all our time triple-testing the chocolate recipes for the first classes as well as devising menus for the guests.'

'But you won't be working on the menus in the evenings, will you? Mm, but who…?' She twisted her lips, her chin still resting in her palm as she stared out into the bay. Millie could almost see the cogs rotating.

'Hey, what time do you call this, Marc!' They heard Andrew's sharp tone slice through the humid air from behind the bar.

'Chill, man,' came the reply. 'It's only six o'clock.'

'Yes, and your shift starts at five. Lottie's had to cover for you again.'

'Lottie doesn't mind. She loves being here. It gives her an excuse to moon after our resident surfer dude.'

'Table five need their bill.' Andrew had clearly decided not to push it. Having just had the conversation with Lottie about going home, he probably didn't want to risk losing two members of staff in one day.

Millie turned her head as Marc appeared on the veranda, stretching his muscular arms over his head as he took in the view of the ocean. Her heart did a somersault and her eyes widened as she took the opportunity to survey him at close quarters. Standing six foot two in his boat shoes, Marc had biceps as firm as his stomach muscles, which were just visible as his white Armani T-shirt rode up his abdomen. He had the looks of a matinee idol from the 1950s. His hair, black as tar, had been carefully gelled into a perfect quiff at his forehead and his come-to-bed eyes drew Millie's attention immediately, sending spasms of desire through her veins.

Unfortunately, Zach had noticed her reaction. He smirked, causing a flush of heat to flood into her face which, coupled with the warmth of the sun blazing overhead, was not a good look. Beetroot was definitely not the new shade of facial foundation.

'Hi, ladies. Thanks for covering for me, Lot. I'll make it up to you.' Marc bent forward to brush a kiss on Lottie's cheek and offer his palm to Zach, who rolled his eyes at being included in the female greeting. Marc then turned his attention to Millie and switched on the charm. 'I don't think we've been introduced. I'm Marc Fisher.'

'Marc, this is Amelia Harper. She's overseeing the renovations at the Croft villa,' said Zach.

'Hi, Amelia.'

'Please. Call me Millie.' She smiled as she met Marc's eyes, framed by the longest lashes she had seen on a man.

'Millie is also the supplier of those dainty little cupcakes that Andy has been handing out to the clientele with their coffee – perfect if you're hosting a birthday party for Barbie's pet unicorn. And careful you don't upset her. She bites.'

'I do not bite!'

Zach leaned forward to deliver a stage whisper to Marc. 'Don't mind her – she's French. Ooops, no, sorry, sorry.' He held up his palm to Millie's face, tossing her a mischievous look. '*Half* French.'

'Which half? Top or bottom?'

Millie saw Lottie shoot a glance at Zach, her eyebrows raised in question, before flicking her eyes over to Marc – she had clearly forgotten about her anxiety over Dylan's flirtation. The corners of her lips turned up with mischief and Millie widened her eyes and shook her head to signal a silent warning to her new friend not to go there, but Lottie ignored her.

'That's three shifts in the last week that you've been late, Marc. You owe me.'

'Hey, chill, Lottie – a guy's got to do what a guy's got to do.'

'And did that involve saying farewell to that Swedish blonde I saw you leave the restaurant with last night?'

'No. I had some business matters to attend to, if you must know. Anyway, I should get to work before Andy spontaneously combusts. Bye, Millie. Great to meet you.' And he strode to the bar, studiously avoiding the stony expression on Andrew's face.

Millie felt herself relax. Marc was handsome and he was definitely her type. But whilst she had decided that she might be ready to start dating again, she didn't want to plunge into those turbulent waters in St Lucia.

Lottie jumped from her chair. 'I've got to go, too. I promised Anisha I'd cover for her in the shop for a couple of hours before I go out tonight. There's a party on at the Blue Oyster if you fancy coming along?'

'Not for me, thanks, Lottie,' said Zach. 'Got some work to catch up on for tomorrow. You should go, though, Millie.'

'No, thanks, Lottie. I want to get back to see how the kitchen fitters have got on today. There's bound to be a mountain of cleaning to catch up on.'

'Hang on a minute then.'

Lottie trotted into the restaurant and leaned over the bar to exchange a few words with Marc. He shot a glance over to where Millie and Zach were finishing off their drinks, flashed his movie-star smile, and nodded.

'All fixed then,' said Lottie as she returned to the table with Zach's change. 'You have a date with Marc next Wednesday night which is his night off. That gives you plenty of time to get ready.'

'Oh, no! Lottie, I really don't…'

'Byeee…'

Zach let out a burst of laughter. 'Shame she's not as proficient at arranging her own love life,' he chuckled, indicating the beach where Dylan had joined Ryan as he headed towards the Purple Parrot.

'Hi, Millie. How's things? Hi, Zach. Just spent a great day out on the *Nigella* diving the reef and exploring the coves out by the marine reserve. Could certainly murder a cold beer!' Dylan slumped into the chair that Lottie had just vacated next to Millie. 'Four Red Stripes, please, Marc.'

'Not for us, thanks, Dylan. We were just leaving, but I'll see you tomorrow.'

'Sure thing. Was that Lottie I saw skipping off?'

'Yes, she's gone to help Anisha with the shop.'

Millie saw Dylan nod as he took a slug of his beer. She tried to interpret his expression but failed.

'Bye.'

Millie wriggled her fingers at Dylan and Ryan and followed Zach to the Roadster for the drive up the hill. Suddenly, her problems with motivating Fitz and his men paled into insignificance when she thought of her forthcoming date with Marc. She was already worrying about what she would wear and whether they would have anything in common, not to mention the fact that there would be an audience at the Purple Parrot watching their every move.

Oh, God! What had she let herself in for?

Chapter Thirteen

'So you reckon it needs more cocoa, not less?'

'Yes, it's not coming through strong enough in the tasting, but a little less on the chillies, they're overpowering the chocolate and it doesn't work,' advised Ella.

It was Tuesday afternoon and a week had passed since Millie's trip to the Diamond Falls. She and Ella had been working in the kitchen all morning on the final few recipes for the start of the Chocolate & Confetti course in six days' time. Everything was coming together well and when they had completed the next batch of chilli-chocolate muffins to Ella's satisfaction they would be finished for the day. Millie was proud of the itinerary Claudia would be offering at the Paradise Cookery School – at least the culinary side of things was on track, ahead of schedule, in fact. She wished she could say the same for the kitchen renovations.

However, for Millie, the best thing about her time in St Lucia had been sharing her passion for food with a fellow baker. She was immensely grateful to Ella for introducing her to unusual Caribbean ingredients and exotic spices, and for demonstrating new techniques. She had listened attentively, consumed every morsel of advice offered, and then put everything into practice with eloquent skill. In a break from the norm, she had used a notebook into which every recipe was copied with her own twists scribbled in the margins.

Then it had been Millie's turn to show Ella some of her signature bakes – a favourite being the gooseberry-and-elderflower millefeuille. Millie experienced a sharp frisson of pride at being given the opportunity to mentor such an accomplished chef. She had never thought anyone would want to listen to what she had to say, let alone so intently and with such obvious gratitude. She was much more accustomed to being the student than the mentor. It was a special feeling.

They had chopped, sautéed, scrambled and poached all week. They had sliced mango, peeled cassava, scooped out passion fruit and grated nutmeg. They had made pineapple jam and lime marmalade, as well as cooked up savoury dishes with yam, okra and plantain. Freshly caught seafood was a special favourite for both of them and they had experimented with barbequing unusual catches offered by the local fishermen only hours from the ocean.

They tasted every recipe they created with a critical palette. The dish had not only to perform magic on their taste buds, but also to produce a feast for the eyes. Herbs, spices, fruits, everything was discussed and catalogued and graded for its ability to add to or deflect from the main ingredients, be it fish, poultry, meat or vegetable.

But the icing on the cake had been their easy camaraderie. They had laughed and giggled as they ate, sharing increasingly intimate details of their lives, their loves, and their dreams for the future.

'I would really love to have a go at presenting a cookery course one day,' mused Millie as she stirred fresh lemon juice into a bowl of powdered sugar.

'Then do it, my dear,' said Ella, slotting the final tray of chocolate muffins into the oven. 'We mould our own destinies, formulate our own dreams. If we don't chase them with single-minded determination, how are they going to come true?'

Ella passed Millie a glass of home-made lime punch made from the remaining limes she had picked from the garden that morning and wandered out to the balcony. The daily deluge had passed and the puddles in the courtyard were rapidly evaporating. The foliage of the banana trees creaked and groaned as the sun resumed its onslaught and the temperature climbed.

'Have you followed your dreams, Ella?' asked Millie quietly, joining her at the railing, sipping from her drink.

'I have. But don't go thinking it's been an easy route. The path to contentment never runs smoothly. It's scattered with boulders the size of pumpkins!'

'What do you mean?'

'I loved Henri's father. Jean-Pierre was in St Lucia for a vacation, but he stayed on – just as you see with many young people who fall in love with our country's beauty. Dylan, Ryan, Lottie, even Andrew who came here at the ripe old age of forty-five – they have all been seduced by our laid-back lifestyle, our friendliness, our acceptance of life's bounty. Everyone is searching for their own version of paradise, but for different reasons and with myriad expectations. Some are escaping trauma, whilst others come seeking personal fulfilment, chasing the elusive dream of experiencing happiness every day of their lives. It takes a long time to understand the truth – that change is internal. Most people simply carry their unresolved issues with them into their new lives expecting things to be different. They rarely are.'

Ella paused, her chestnut eyes misting as she thought back to her time with Henri's father. 'We partied, we swam, we danced on the beach in the moonlight. We begged a boat and searched for secluded coves where we could make love. He was my soulmate. I was twenty-two and I had never loved anyone as much – nor since.'

'So what happened?'

'It's simple. I fell pregnant. That wasn't on the agenda. Jean-Pierre had a life in France. I don't think he'd thought beyond the palm trees and the sunshine and the golden beaches. He certainly hadn't contemplated living in the Caribbean permanently with a native of the islands. Oh, I don't think it was a cultural issue. We both spoke fluent French, we were both Catholics. No, I just don't think having a family was on his radar at that time in his life – having a child anywhere, in fact. He panicked and caught the next flight home. I never set eyes on him again.'

Millie could think of no words to ease the pain etched on her friend's gentle face, even after all these years. Henri had told her he was twenty-eight, and still a holiday romance had the ability to scar for life.

'But didn't Henri study at a French university?' asked Millie.

'Yes, he did. It was hard being a single parent, not only financially – there was a stigma attached to being an unmarried mother, especially after a fling with a holidaymaker! I never thought of our relationship as a fling because I had truly loved Jean-Pierre. But we managed, despite the orchestrator of my fate not having the decency to provide me with a variety of options.'

The smooth chocolate of her skin, strong, rounded cheekbones and proud tilt of her chin belied the vagaries of a life lived as a lone parent prepared to do whatever necessary to make a better life for her son, despite the accident of his birth.

'Henri got a job helping out at the newspaper when he was fourteen and that kept him in pocket money and out of trouble. It's so difficult for young people today, especially the boys. There's such pressure to hang out with the gangs, get involved in drugs, even guns. I couldn't let that happen to my Henri so I gathered my courage and contacted Jean-Pierre. It's easier nowadays with social media. I found him without any problem and he was doing very well for himself too. An equine vet in Bordeaux, no less. Anyway, he agreed to sponsor Henri whilst he did his degree in France.

'I had told Henri everything as he was growing up so it wasn't a surprise. I think he did meet his father a few times whilst he was over there, but they never managed to build a relationship. Henri loved France, especially Paris, but he was always eager to catch the flight back home in the summer holidays. Every year he resumed his job at the Soufrière *Tribune* until he graduated. I think he has plans to be editor-in-chief one day.'

The pride in her son's achievements shone from Ella's plump face. It was clear she adored him, but it was much more than that; she respected him, and Millie knew it was reciprocated.

'Talking of romance,' said Ella. 'What are you planning to wear for your date with Marc tomorrow night?'

'Oh, I'm not even sure I'm going to go.'

'Why not?'

'I… I don't think I'm ready to step on the dating carousel yet, that's all.'

'Well, far be it from me to say that it's just a little bit of holiday fun!' Ella laughed.

Millie smiled at her friend, and was grateful that Ella didn't push her for an explanation. She knew that it was the perfect time to share her story, but she wasn't ready. Since her arrival in St Lucia she had felt as though real life had been suspended, that she was living in an alternate dimension; one that did not include infidelity or heartache. She was enjoying being with people who saw her for who she was, not what had happened to her, and she wanted to extend that feeling for as long as possible. She knew Ella would forgive her reticence.

So, if this was another world, then why shouldn't she have a night out with Marc? Did it matter how it turned out? They both knew that she was going back to the UK in a few days' time so what did she have to lose?

She smiled at Ella. 'I've got a lovely peach-and-cream sundress. Shall I try it on?'

'Absolutely!'

Millie's spirits edged up a notch and she realized she was actually looking forward to her no-strings-attached date.

Chapter Fourteen

With only three full work days left, including Friday – the scheduled completion day – Millie had to reluctantly admit that the renovations were seriously behind schedule. She had employed every technique in her armoury, every argument, every inducement, every method of persuasion she could think of. She had even resorted to baking a selection of mouth-watering French pastries to cajole the trio of artisans into upping their speed from plodding to at least rolling. But nothing she did or said succeeded in increasing their work rate. The gear stick was well and truly stuck on dawdle.

Every day they arrived in the courtyard to the accompaniment of a Bob Marley classic at eight a.m., instead of the required seven. It was so hot in the middle of the day that the extra hour in the morning was vital to progress. She couldn't blame them for breaking for lunch, relaxing either on the sunloungers on the terrace or taking a snooze in the back of their van until two o'clock when the sun had burned its brightest. Occasionally they would disappear home for their lunch – or so Millie had naively assumed. She had been informed by an irate Ella the previous day that they were spending their two hours away from the villa in a bar on the road to Soufrière. She should have realized, given Vic's propensity to drop his tools in the pool on his return.

She had spoken to Fitz that morning about the slippage in the schedule, tried to impress upon him how important it was to get the kitchen finished. He had listened to her litany of suggestions with a serene expression, the habitual cigarette dangling from his lips, a pencil behind his ear, but had simply shrugged and told her to relax.

'But Fitz, there are six wedding guests arriving on Monday and they will be expecting a high-spec, professional-standard kitchen which is pristine – and safe! Claudia's reputation is on the line, never mind her money.' However, Millie knew the words 'deadline' and 'schedule' and 'rush' would never appear on Fitz's Scrabble board.

'No problem, Millie.'

'We're at least two days behind!' she had cried, but Fitz simply met her desperate pleading with a slow, languid smile and patted her on the arm before turning the radio up, sucking on his unlit cigarette like a toddler on his dummy. Apparently, Wednesday was a big night out and the guys had spent the whole day chattering about their plans for the evening in a selection of Castries's infamous bars.

A helix of panic had escalated with each passing day as she surveyed the progress when Fitz, Alph and Vic left for the evening. She knew the delay was her fault and an uncomfortable ball of dread nestled in the pit of her stomach.

At least she was happy with the culinary progress. She and Ella had most of the recipes sorted and what a fabulous selection there was. Waves of excitement crashed through her as she rolled through the list of exotic dishes in her mind. All finalized recipes had been emailed to Claudia who was holed up, bored to distraction in her bedroom at her manor house in the Cotswolds. She was always eager to hear their suggestions for tweaking her recipes. After the operation to pin her ankle the doctors had prescribed her such potent painkillers that she had confessed to not feeling in complete control of her faculties and had told them to trust their instincts and she would accept their judgement. When Millie had questioned whether she would be fit enough to fly out to St Lucia at the weekend, Claudia had assured her that she would be and it was a brave medic that would keep her away.

So, at least the cookery school part of things would be ready. If only she could be as confident about Fitz delivering on his kitchen promise, she would be able to enjoy her adventure in the Caribbean a whole lot more. As the men were currently indulging in their daily siesta, Millie decided to take the opportunity to wash down the paintwork and the marble floor and do whatever she could to get a head start on the finishing touches.

She grabbed a cleaning cloth and a brush and skipped across the courtyard to the villa's back door. Again, a jolt of surprise hit her. Just that morning she had purposely stacked the empty wooden crates and bamboo basket in the shed behind the garage to remove any further possibility of having to question her sanity. But here they were, back in their usual place on the doorstep, two of them, with the basket perched on the top filled with cocoa pods. Now she *knew* something was going on. She resolved to speak to Fitz the following day as it could only be one of his gang who had done this – possibly as a joke, but it wasn't funny any more.

She opened the concertinaed glass doors and stood on the veranda to survey the kitchen. It *would* be spectacular. The skeleton was in place – the run of worktops in front of the windows to take full advantage of the view, the huge stainless-steel professional-grade oven, the enormous SMEG fridge-freezer standing to attention on the back wall, the marble-topped island unit at the centre of the room – minus its sink and taps – from where Claudia would present her Paradise Cookery School courses.

There was space for two students at each of the four workbenches, which had their own sinks, swan-necked taps and electric ovens. A white granite-topped table had been delivered the previous day and would easily accommodate the course tutor and eight diners sitting down to sample their creations at the end of the day.

Millie set about polishing the table and the countertops, then moved on to brush the floor free of sawdust and splodges of plaster and glue. The carcases had no doors. There were no wall units, no skirting boards fitted, and the wall tiles still had to be grouted. A squirm of discomfort reinforced the fear that there was a real risk the project would not be completed on time. There was no way they could accept paying guests into a work-in-progress.

She ditched her cloth and scoured the room for her favourite appliance – a Fracino Retro coffee machine. Every item that had been delivered had been unpacked and most of the appliances were in place. But she couldn't see the coffee machine anywhere. It wasn't difficult to perform a search as the cupboards were all open. She scoured the larder, whose shelves were bare save for a pile of handles and hinges. Then she sauntered down the corridor to the six bedrooms; nothing.

An unpleasant thought entered her head. She had definitely seen the box and now it was missing. Just like the cocoa pods. Was there more to the mysterious disappearances than she was giving credit for? Okay, the pods had no value, but a commercial-grade coffee machine was a different league. Should she share her concerns with Claudia? First the obvious delay in the schedule, and now the possibility of a theft of the appliances she was responsible for?

Millie's throat tightened around a knot of anxiety that had nothing to do with the fact that the renovations were behind schedule. Perhaps unwisely, she had told Poppy about her date with Marc and her friend was so excited about her first foray into the dating game since they had met that she had been emailing and texting her every couple of hours with tips on what to wear and what to talk about on a first date.

Yet Poppy was right. She should be looking forward to spending time with such an attractive and charismatic guy. The gnawing sensation in her stomach was just nerves because her confidence in the field of romance had taken a battering. She had to believe that she was ready to move on unless she wanted to end up as a lonely old spinster and there was no way she was going to let Luke do that to her.

Anyway, what better time to dip her toe in the water than whilst away from the normal routine with someone she was unlikely to see again? Her date with Marc that evening was a great way to break the monotony of her celibacy. If she didn't go for a drink with Marc, when would she get the chance to go on a date next? She never met anyone in London – she was always too busy at the patisserie.

Millie returned to her studio and decided to follow Fitz's example and take a short siesta herself. When she woke, the men had left for the day and she only had an hour before she had to be at the Purple Parrot. She hopped in the shower and luxuriated in the cool cascade that reminded her of the waterfall she had visited the previous week. She styled her voluminous hair with coconut oil and even painted her fingernails – something she rarely did as a chef.

She drained the glass of Prosecco she had poured for Dutch courage and stepped into her peach-and-cream sundress – a new addition to her wardrobe courtesy of Lottie's friend Anisha. She had also made her a beautiful necklace from tiny peach-and-cream shells and as she fastened it around her neck, Millie felt as though the whole of the Purple Parrot was involved in her date. With a final glance in the mirror, she grabbed her bag and trotted down the stairs.

Marc wouldn't stand her up – would he?

Chapter Fifteen

Millie locked the door of her studio and, out of habit, glanced across at the crates on the step, expecting them to be filled to the top – just as they had been when she returned from the villa earlier. In a split second, she not only noticed that the boxes were empty but caught a glimpse of a jeep's red tail lights disappearing around the end of the driveway. Without thinking she gave chase.

'Hey! Hey! Stop!'

The jeep did not stop. If anything, the driver increased their speed. But it didn't matter – she had recognized the vehicle. She shook her head as she made her way down the hill towards where a taxi waited to take her to the town and her rendezvous with Marc at the Purple Parrot, unable to believe what she had just seen.

Why was Dylan stealing Claudia's cocoa pods? It didn't make any sense. He ran a diving school, not a restaurant or a bar.

She hopped into the back of the cab and stared up at the sky. It was not the usual expanse of inky black dotted with an infinity of stars, but leaden, with steel-grey clouds pressing down on the twin peaks of the Pitons, their flanks soaring dark, high and foreboding. The wind had increased and, whilst she appreciated the fresh whisper of salty air flowing through the open windows, she sensed a storm was brewing out at sea. A shiver ran the length of her spine and she was grateful to duck into the welcome hospitality of the Purple Parrot.

Her preoccupation with the kitchen and her unease about Dylan had pushed any lingering nerves about her date from her mind, especially when she spotted Dylan drinking a beer at the bar with Ryan. Lottie leaned over the varnished top, hanging on his every word. Clearly her threat to move back home to the UK was on hold for the time being. Her hair rippled like burgundy wine down past her shoulders and she wore a gathered, white linen, gypsy-style blouse and a pair of very short shorts.

Millie studied Dylan's face in profile, searching his expression for an indication that he knew she had seen him at the villa. Nothing – just a wide-open, friendly smile. His Hawaiian shirt would have looked ridiculous anywhere else, but with his tousled hair, denim shorts and tanned forearms, he looked every inch the classic beach boy: attractive, happy and relaxed in his own skin. She could understand Lottie's love for this man, but the question still remained – why on earth was he stealing Claudia's cocoa pods?

She glanced around the veranda but there was no sign of Marc. Instead of joining Lottie and Dylan, she decided to grab a seat overlooking the beachfront. After a few minutes of waiting, a swirl of apprehension started to curl around her stomach. Would he come? Had he changed his mind about taking her out for dinner? She didn't think she could stand the collective sympathy of the Purple Parrot if that were the case. She slid her mobile from her bag and glanced at the screen – no messages.

'Want a drink while you wait?' asked Andrew, holding up a glass, unable to meet her eyes.

Oh, God! thought Millie. Andrew knew that Marc wasn't coming and that was why he'd brought a cocktail outside to her to soften the blow he was about to deliver. She glanced at the lacklustre attempt at a daiquiri he set on the table in front of her, minus the usual embellishment of a slice of lime or parrot-topped cocktail stick or sugared rim. She offered him a nervous smile and saw from his face that he wore the stress of his financial difficulties heavily around his eyes and in the sag of his shoulders. It was a worrying time for many businesses that relied on the tourist dollar or pound or euro, and the Purple Parrot was no exception. Andrew turned his back without uttering an exchange and strode back to the kitchen.

'Don't mind him, Millie. He had a meeting at the bank yesterday,' whispered Lottie, appearing at the table, her eyes trained on the door through which Andrew had disappeared. 'The manager refused to extend his overdraft. Apparently, the restaurant's been running on empty for the last year. There's a chance he could lose the business. And one thing I do know is that he doesn't want to go crawling back to the rain-splattered streets of Oldham.'

'I can totally understand that! There's no comparison.'

'Not just that, though.' Lottie checked Andrew was still safely ensconced in the kitchen. 'He was made bankrupt before he came over here. His wife left him destitute after their divorce, he couldn't pay his bills and his restaurant folded. So he *can't* go back. He has to make the Purple Parrot work. Only, I'm not sure what his options are.'

Millie could see that Andrew O'Leary was one of those unfortunate people who couldn't allow themselves to be happy and carried a mantle of melancholy throughout their lives — even when surrounded by paradise. To the casual onlooker, Andrew was living the dream — certainly owning a bar overlooking golden sands and the magnificence of the St Lucian Pitons was Millie's dream. What a waste.

But wasn't that exactly what she had been doing for the last six months? Yet another of life's lessons was delivered with a sharp slap to her face.

'Don't tell him I said anything, but he's been like a rampaging lion all day. He disappeared for an hour earlier without a word and when he got back it was obvious he'd been drinking — lots!' Lottie cast a worried glance over her shoulder at the kitchen door.

'I see our friend Marc's not a man to impress his date with his timekeeping,' said Dylan, arriving at the table and slotting his arm around Lottie's shoulders, producing a wide grin.

'Actually, perhaps it's just as well. I think I'll…'

'Oh, no, Millie, you can't bail yet. Marc's always late for everything. He'll be here. He promised. It's just a drink, then maybe a meal, and a stroll along the beach in the moonlight, hand in hand…'

'Don't think that would be wise, Lot. There's a tropical storm on its way – Category two. You've heard the warnings to stay indoors after ten p.m. Look, the wind's already getting up.' Dylan gestured towards the beach where the waves galloped across the dark surface of the water like a cavalry in full battle-mode.

'Oh, okay… then perhaps you could go back to his place, hide out from the storm, listening to the rain cascade down the roof tiles as he encircles you in his strong, muscular arms, sheltering you from…'

'Lottie, please shut up,' Millie giggled, taking a gulp of her cocktail.

'Love is the answer, Millie!' Dylan laughed before his face grew more serious. 'Just be careful, that's all. Marc has a reputation with the ladies. You need to know he's not in it for the long term.'

'It's just a drink, Dylan,' Millie smiled, grateful for his concern, even more confused about his actions earlier before blurting, 'Did you lend your jeep to anyone this evening, Dylan?'

'Hey, Dylan. Can I borrow you for a minute?' called Andrew, poking his nose around the kitchen door, his eyes bulging with tiredness, his bandana in need of a good wash and press.

'Sure, Andy, I'll be right there. Good luck, Millie. Enjoy your date. And remember about the storm. Make sure Marc gets you home safely. You don't want to be climbing that hill alone in the rain.'

'Love is the answer, he says!' spluttered Lottie, putting a second cocktail in front of Millie who hadn't realized she'd finished the first. This one had all the trimmings and she relished the zing on her taste buds. 'I wish he'd take his own advice.'

'Millie! Millie! Sorry I'm late. A Red Stripe and whatever Millie is having please, Lottie.'

Marc's appearance squashed all the intentions Millie had of reprimanding him for not being on time. He looked like a polished Greek Adonis. His black dress trousers fit him snugly around the buttocks, belted at his trim waist. His matching D&G shirt was open at the neck to reveal just a hint of chest hair. And he smelled delicious. She inhaled the mixture of wood spice and cloves and an arrow of desire shot to her stomach and travelled south. His brown eyes smouldered and she melted.

'You look gorgeous,' said Marc, staring straight into her eyes when he spoke and leaning down to peck her on the cheek before taking the seat opposite her.

A cauldron of emotions rushed through her veins as she anticipated the night ahead. He was handsome, confident in his own golden-tanned skin, and proved to be an attentive companion.

Millie sipped on the daiquiri mixed by Lottie and stared at the churning sea delivering thick ribbons of froth to the beach whilst the moon played hide-and-seek with the heavy clouds scooting across the sky. Palm trees fringed the scene, bent so low under the strengthening wind that Millie thought they would touch the sand. The mats and napkins on the outdoor wooden tables flapped so vigorously that the diners abandoned their attempts of a romantic dinner à deux under the stars and retreated into the restaurant.

Marc went to order another round of drinks from the bar, speaking to Andrew instead of calling Lottie over to their table. She watched him cast his eyes over his shoulder to look at her and then continue in a sweep around the restaurant taking in everyone who was there. A squirm of annoyance writhed in her chest. Was he checking the room for his next conquest? But she chastised herself. Marc didn't owe her anything. This was only a drink.

The rum scorched through Millie's veins and the conversation flowed. It turned out that they had a great deal in common, liked the same films, even shared a love of rugby. Marc told her he had worked at the Purple Parrot since the previous summer season and before that at numerous bars in Antigua, Martinique and Jamaica. He also revealed that he had a connection with Andrew, a second cousin or something, Millie couldn't remember as her attention was taken up by his chocolate-brown eyes and the proximity of his muscular body. The guy oozed charisma. Every time his hand brushed hers an electrical pulse shot through her veins.

The cocktails slipped down easily. She was enjoying herself immensely and when Marc suggested they go and eat she followed him out of the bar, a wide grin on her face, tripping over the kerb and forcing her to grab on to his arm. They walked hand in hand to a secluded backstreet restaurant filled to bursting with locals enjoying their evening out.

Marc ordered for them both, which Millie was a little surprised about, but she let it go. She was happy to try anything on offer in the rough-around-the-edges restaurant, complete with live band playing reggae tunes at full blast and a tantalizing aroma of roast chicken. As they waited for their starters to arrive, the conversation dried up and Millie realized that she was more than a little tipsy. She cast around for something to say and went with the first thing that came into her head.

'How well do you know Dylan?'

'Fairly well. Great guy.' Marc sipped his beer, his eyes resting on hers.

'It's just, well, I'm not sure whether I should say anything…'

'What's the problem?'

'I know it's nothing really, but over the last week a stack of cocoa pods has been disappearing from the villa. At first I thought I was going crazy, but tonight I saw Dylan's jeep speed away down the hill and another crate had been emptied.'

'Did you actually see it was him? There're a lot of jeeps around here, you know.'

'I'm certain. I know the pods are worthless, but it's strange, don't you think? What would Dylan want with a few dozen cocoa pods? It's not as though he's into cooking!'

'Have you said anything to him about it?'

'No. I thought about it, but then you arrived and…'

'I'm sure you must have been mistaken, Millie.'

'Do you think I should mention it to Henri? He's friends with Leon, the police sergeant in Soufrière.'

'No, I wouldn't do that. Those pods would have probably been left to rot, anyway. I'm sure Claudia doesn't mind anyone helping themselves.'

'But why wouldn't he say what he was doing? Why did he speed away when he saw me? It doesn't make any sense.'

Their meal arrived – red snapper stuffed with chopped spring onion and tomato salsa that had been doused with soy and ginger and wrapped in banana leaves, and another rum cocktail for Millie. She ate very little, giddy with the alcohol and Marc's attentive company. The humidity and reggae music swirled around her head and she felt mellow and attractive under Marc's gaze, as if he had cast a spell of enchantment over their evening. She was surprised to find that she craved his touch on her arm, on her neck, her cheek. The pounding of her heart, insistent on the continuance of these welcome emotions, blotted out all sense and prudence.

The music stopped and so did the conversation as a loud crack of thunder hurtled down from the sky. The gathering laughed and the chatter resumed as a second flash of lightning sliced through the open frontage of the restaurant.

'Dylan mentioned there would be a tropical storm tonight,' said Millie before throwing caution to the wind. 'Why don't we ditch the dessert course and go back to the villa for a nightcap before the rain arrives?'

'Sounds… Oh, hang on.' Marc extracted his phone from his pocket. 'Excuse me, I need to take this.' He left his seat and strode out through the back door of the restaurant.

Millie finished her cocktail. She had lost count of how many she'd had. She reached down to grab her handbag and, giggling to herself, stumbled to the Ladies' to splash cold water on her face. She looked at herself in the mirror. Her cheeks were like two ripe tomatoes and her hair was springing out from her head like a clown on speed. She groaned, running her fingers through the tresses to straighten them.

As she peeped out through the back door of the restaurant down the alleyway, another crack of lightning lit the sky. Huge raindrops splashed down onto the tarmac and she expected to see Marc finishing off his conversation, but he was nowhere in sight.

Must be back at the table, she thought. She decided that it might be a good idea if they stayed for coffee, not only to avoid the deluge, but so she could sober up before they left. When she arrived at the table Marc wasn't there either. She glanced around the room, but he wasn't chatting to any of the clientele or the owner. She waited a few more minutes and when he didn't materialize, she strolled out to the street and scoured the road to the left and the right and then, again, the alleyway.

Nothing.

She stood on the doorstep, watching the storm, a sense of unease mounting. Where was Marc? He couldn't still be on the phone, nor could he have visited the Gents' for such a long time. She looked at her watch and saw he had been gone for over twenty minutes.

The fuzziness in her head was starting to clear. She pushed her way back into the restaurant and found the waiter who had taken their order.

'Erm, have you seen Marc... my date?'

'No, ma'am. Sorry.'

'Oh, erm, okay, thanks.'

Millie didn't know what to do next. She rifled in her bag for her purse and left more than enough dollars to cover the cost of the meal. She fiddled with her empty cocktail glass for ten more minutes and then left the restaurant by the back door, stumbling down the alleyway to the front street, but still there was no sign of Marc.

She checked her phone. Nothing. Glad they'd exchanged numbers, she tapped out a text, uncertain whether to be worried or annoyed. Had he had such an abysmal evening with her that he'd done a runner?

Oh, God! Her stomach contracted violently. It was the same scenario as she had endured with Luke at their engagement party. Was it even statistically possible that lightning could strike the same person twice in exactly the same way?

To answer her rhetorical question, the meteorological gods confirmed their answer by sending down a violent crack of light in front of her. Another cacophonous rumble of thunder followed and the fronds of the palm trees lining the road leaned so far over that it looked like a foliage tunnel. Reluctantly she came to the conclusion that there was nothing else she could do except make her way back to the Purple Parrot and ask Lottie to order a taxi to take her home.

Chapter Sixteen

'Oh, my God, Millie. What's happened? Where's Marc? Why do you look like a drowned rat?' Lottie shot from her position behind the bar and steered Millie into a cane chair at the back of the restaurant. It was after midnight and the majority of the Purple Parrot's customers had retired to their villas and apartments to shelter from the storm.

'Can you call me a taxi, please, Lottie?' Millie muttered as an onslaught of trembling overtook her. She had opened her heart to being bruised again and just look what had happened. Bruised? Ha! Sliced open with a cleaver. Dating was a mug's game and she had no intention of ever, ever securing a rematch! She had never been brilliant at choosing a life companion, but once again she had scraped the bottom of the barrel.

'Of course I'll call you a taxi, but I think you need a brandy first.' Lottie's pale blue eyes widened with concern and she was back at Millie's side with a glass of Andrew's best cognac in seconds. 'Tell me what happened! Why aren't you with Marc?'

Millie sipped the brandy and felt the warmth trickle down into her chest, calming her raging emotions enough for her to utter, 'He ditched me.'

'What do you mean, he ditched you?'

'After we finished our meal, he left to take a call and never came back.'

'He what?!'

Millie met Lottie's eyes and the pity she saw reflected there sent tears to her own. But she grabbed on to her emotions – she was determined not to cry until she was alone in her studio where no one could see her. After all, it was only a date with a guy she hardly knew. He was not Luke – the man she had thought she was going to marry! But Lottie didn't know any of this so she dragged up every ounce of courage she could and forced a smile on her lips.

'Perhaps his call was an emergency.' muttered Millie.

'But he should have told you!'

'Maybe.'

'Wait until I…'

Thankfully, Millie didn't have to hear how Lottie planned to punish Marc for his ungentlemanly behaviour as Clavie had arrived at the door, his eyes searching the room for his client.

'See you later, Lottie.'

'Hang on. I'll ask Andy if I can come with you. You shouldn't be alone tonight after what's happened.'

'Oh, no, Lottie, you don't have to do that. I'm fine. It's not as though Marc and I are an item or anything. It was just two people having dinner. Look, I promise to come down for breakfast in the morning and we can chat about what happened at our leisure.'

'Well, if you're sure...' Lottie's ski-slope nose crinkled in doubt.

'I'm sure. Thanks for the brandy. It was exactly what I needed. Bye.'

Millie gave Lottie a quick hug, and dashed outside to the taxi. The storm had passed but the rain was still lashing down with abandon on the town's rooftops. She slid into the back seat and Clavie, who probably possessed some kind of sixth sense, drove quickly and in silence up the hill towards the villa. As she had expected, he stopped at the bottom of the driveway.

'Sorry, Millie.'

'It's okay, Clavie. I'll be fine. Thanks.'

She shoved a few notes into his hand, anxious to escape into her thoughts. She watched the red tail lights disappeared and turned to make her way up the drive. She had taken only a couple of paces when the full blast of her predicament engulfed her senses and she burst into huge racking sobs. Her tears mingled with the raindrops that were falling like glass spears onto the wide-brimmed foliage above her head, making her feel even worse. She scrambled around in her bag for a tissue, but within seconds it was a sodden mess of paper.

A parrot launched itself from the treetops and she screamed, but the sound was swallowed into the shadows and extinguished. She hurled herself up the incline, gulping in mouthfuls of soup-like air. The humidity and overwhelming intensity of nature's bounty threatened to overwhelm her. A cathedral of arboreal magnificence in the daylight it might be, but under the mantle of darkness it had morphed into a macabre pantomime of horrors in whose wings danced terror and fear. Was there a brigade of nocturnal animals roaming the forest waiting to pounce on her and maul her to death?

Yet the birds continued to twitter their night-time sonata, unaware of the panic burgeoning in their midst, and by the time she reached the courtyard her thoughts had spiralled into another sphere of enquiry.

Why had Marc abandoned her at the restaurant? What had she ever done to him to deserve such inconsiderate treatment?

None of it made any sense and no matter which way she framed the questions, the treasure trove of answers was empty. And was it any wonder? The whole evening had been a catalogue of mysteries and strange behaviour. First Dylan acting as though nothing had happened despite her running after the jeep, shaking her hands in the air like a demented cheerleader, when he screeched away with his stash of worthless cocoa pods. Then Marc vanishing into thin air when all he had to do was tell her he wasn't interested in a second date!

Millie was so absorbed in chasing her confusion down blind alleyways that she didn't hear the purr of an engine approach her from behind and had she been of a more nervous disposition she would have needed mouth-to-mouth resuscitation when a car horn blasted from two feet away.

'Hey, Princess Cupcake! Need a warm fire and a nightcap?'

Millie had never been so relieved to see anyone in her life. She rushed towards Tim's Roadster and jumped into the passenger seat. 'Oh, Zach, you have no idea how pleased I am to see you,' and she promptly burst into tears.

Zach remained silent during the five minutes it took to drive to his lodge in the grounds of the plantation. They lurched and leapt along the deep furrows of the earthen track like an excitable kangaroo, before finally skirting a fringe of tropical forest crammed with a brigade of banana trees. An ivory moon appeared from behind the clouds and bathed the landscape in a mottled aura. It looked like a scene staged for a movie, but Millie felt as though she had landed a role in the horror genre rather than the romance genre.

Zach's home could best be described as an old steamer boat moored against a dense arboreal backdrop. A wraparound wooden veranda gave the impression of a ship's gangways, which afforded a spectacular outlook over the whole estate. Clad in a mantle of vapour, the topography of the grounds had been obscured, but in the distance the peaks of the Pitons reared majestically above the sea, now calm and smooth like a piece of crumpled black tinfoil. Any film director would be delighted at the cinematography of the setting. It was Oscar-winning.

'Come on. Let's get you warmed up. And before you ask, Lottie called me. She was worried about you. She also told me what happened with Marc so you don't have to rehash any of the sorry tale if you don't want to.'

A concerto of excited barking sprang from behind the door as Zach grappled with the lock.

'Okay, Binks, behave. We have a visitor.'

Zach grabbed the dog's collar and fondled his silky ears before leading him to his tartan-lined basket next to the fireplace and settling him down with a reassuring pat and a dog biscuit from his pocket. He crossed to the wood-burning stove, chucked a couple of logs from the wire basket inside and lit a fire – just being with Zach had calmed her serrated nerves and soothed her soul. How did he do that?

'Grab a seat and I'll make us some coffee.'

Millie did as she was told and watched Zach open one of the cupboards in search of a jar of coffee. Even in Étienne's kitchen she had not met with such meticulous organization. She wasn't surprised to see an array of jars of varying exoticness – spices, herbs, flavoured salts. It was the fact that every last label faced the front that shocked her – and she had come across her share of obsessive chefs. It was like a supermodel's closet – winter, spring, summer, each item colour coordinated with handbag and shoes. She couldn't resist further investigation.

'Are these in alphabetical order?'

Zach removed the spice jar from her hand, returned it to its rightful place, and shooed her off into the sitting room.

'Go and sit next to the fire and keep Binks company.'

Whilst Zach clattered around the tiny kitchen making coffee, Millie took the opportunity to survey the lounge area. Like the kitchen, the room was so tidy it squeaked. A display of intricately carved objects marched across the shelves above the fireplace and colourful, framed local artwork hung on the walls. A pair of high-tech binoculars lounging on the windowsill was the only item that seemed out of place.

To the left of the stove stood a floor-to-ceiling bookcase, its occupants inserted in meticulous descending order. Millie knew you could glean a great deal about a person from their reading material and was curious to know what type of books Zach preferred. *Caring for Cocoa? Tropical Forest Management Techniques? The Art of Polite Conversation?*

The warmth of the fire began to weave ribbons of comfort around her limbs and seep into her bones. The crackling of the logs and the rhythmic, flickering flames were mesmerizing. She stared unblinking into its depths as tiny tumbles of ash dribbled from the grate to the hearth like silver confetti. She relaxed into the crumpled leather sofa – one of a pair perfectly placed at right angles to the burner, separated by a pale blue, geometric-patterned rug more befitting a New York loft than a Caribbean lodge. Millie couldn't prevent a giggle from escaping her lips.

'What?' asked Zach, handing her a mug laced with a tot of rum.

'It's just that I expected the floor coverings to be animal skins – you know, with a bear or a tiger's head? But perhaps not – that would have interfered with the smooth lines of the pared-back "hunter's paradise" theme you're working here.'

'Just because I work outdoors doesn't mean I have to live in a scuzzy hut! As a matter of fact, Messy Millie, I can't stand the domestic turmoil you seem to thrive in. I need to know where every-thing is. It's good karma to be organized – it frees up brain space for the important things in life.'

'And what are they?' Millie realized she knew very little about the man who had prepared freshly ground coffee like a professional alchemist. He continually surprised her – she'd expected instant

Nescafé. Now that she had the time to study him in his home environment she saw how attractive he was with his ebony hair, neatly teased into spikes, his jawline smooth and stubble free, and the thickest of liquorice-coloured eyelashes

'Well, ensuring the smooth running of the estate for a start. Nature needs to be constantly tamed otherwise chaos will reign. It's a never-ending task – there's always something to do. Usually I'm out of the door at six a.m. and not back until dusk.'

'So have you always worked in estate management?' Millie asked, sipping her coffee, anxious to avoid the elephant in the room for as long as possible.

'I love working outdoors. When I was growing up I spent every waking hour with my brother down at the local beck, damming up the stream with rocks and branches – proper pair of little beavers we were. I could name every species of bird and every variety of plant before I was eight years old. But when I was ten Mum and Dad moved to London so Dad could take up a management position at one of the largest international law firms in the capital.'

Millie saw Zach's jaw tighten and his eyes drop, his face a mask belying the intensity of his pain. 'It must have been tough to leave the countryside for the urban sprawl of London. Leaving all your friends behind.' Something she totally understood.

'It was particularly hard on Mum at first. But Dad's new job paid well. We lived in a large Victorian terrace in Pimlico and his firm subsidized my and my brother Callum's school fees. What we lost in freedom we gained in academic excellence. Mum settled eventually, though. She adored the West End theatres, even landed a few regular roles as an extra in a couple of hospital dramas and sitcoms. But she worked mainly as a legal secretary and later on as a paralegal.'

'And are your parents still in London?'

'Dad is. With his new girlfriend. One of the solicitors in his law firm – twenty years his junior. Mum was devastated when she found out about his infidelity, but her vanity wouldn't allow her to acquire the role of the pitied, scorned partner. So she moved back to rural Oxfordshire.' Zach swallowed the last sip of coffee and grimaced at the bitter taste.

'So have you worked for Tim and Claudia since university?' Millie pressed, wondering if his answer would provide an insight into his obsessive craving for neatness, his compelling need for order in all aspects of his life.

'Yes. I leapt at the chance when the position of estate manager at their Cotswolds manor house became vacant. Spending every working day in the fresh air is as close to career satisfaction as you can get. When Claudia told me about their plans to offer archery classes as well as quad bike and Segway trekking to the Cotswold Cookery School students, it was a done deal.'

'Do you think they'll extend the same activities to the Paradise Cookery School students?'

'Definitely. In fact, I plan to offer a couple of taster sessions on the quad bikes to the guys whilst the girls enjoy the Chocolate & Confetti course next week. Claudia and Tim are hoping the plantation will take off as wedding venue too.'

'Well, it's certainly a fairy-tale setting.'

'I thought you'd say that. Yes, there's obviously an abundance of sunshine, swaying palm trees, golden beaches and as much rum punch as you can sail a yacht in. It *is* a paradise, but believe it or not, Little Miss Sunshine, some people adore the Cotswolds or the Lake District or the Scottish Highlands. Those are their dream wedding locations – some couples even want to get hitched in a yurt under a canopy of stars. It's romantic. Heard of that concept?'

'Of course I've heard of romance! Actually, the French are masters of romance and love!'

Zach held her eyes and her stomach gave an uncomfortable lurch. They had arrived at the point in their conversation where she spilled out the whole sorry story, not only of her date with Marc, but what had happened with Luke. Zach had been open and honest about his life whilst they sheltered in the little wooden hut on the slopes of the Pitons, but she had chickened out. She couldn't do that again.

In fact, she didn't want to. She was looking forward to sharing her past with him – warts and all. She had never experienced such a barrage of intense emotion as she was experiencing at that moment, not with Luke or anyone else before him, and she felt alive for the first time in years. She curled her legs under her bottom, hugged her mug to her chest and launched into an abridged version of the shambles she had made of her life to date.

'The reason I was so upset about Marc abandoning me at the restaurant was because it's not the first time I've been summarily ditched. It felt like history was repeating itself, but of course, my date with Marc was nothing like what happened with Luke.'

She paused as the whole episode came rushing back at her with a vengeance.

'Six months ago, at the beginning of April, my boyfriend, sorry, my soon-to-be fiancé, broke off our engagement. Oh, he didn't break the news face to face or in a phone call, or even by text. No, he just didn't turn up at our engagement party so I had to endure the humiliation of being dumped in front of all our friends and family. I didn't see it coming and was devastated. When I eventually managed to speak to him to ask him why, he told me that he had met someone else.'

Millie gulped down a mouthful of coffee and stared into the embers of the wood-burning stove. She couldn't look at Zach, didn't want to see the pity on his face.

'It was a nightmare because we co-managed a Michelin-starred restaurant in Oxford. At first I thought that he should be the one to leave. After all, it had been his choice to cheat on me and throw our future away. But when I discovered the identity of the other woman, there was no way I could stay – not at the restaurant, not even in Oxford.'

'Why not?'

Millie didn't hear Zach's question. She had already been transported back to that harrowing time after her world had ground to a halt.

'Of course, I shared everything with my best friend Frankie, everything. She was so supportive, so angry with Luke. It was Frankie who found out who his new girlfriend was, and I honestly think she was more shocked and horrified than I was.'

She paused, gathering her courage to deliver the final sentence, the sentence that until now she had only uttered to her mother and Jen. Even Poppy thought Luke had run off with some random girl.

'Luke had been having an affair with Frankie's mother for six months. They are expecting their first child in January.'

There it was: a neat summary of her life in a few carefully chosen words but surprisingly without the expected gush of self-indulgent tears. Memories of the day Frankie had appeared on her doorstep, her face as grey as overworked pastry, still haunted her dreams. Until she had arrived in St Lucia, she frequently woke up with damp cheeks – the physical evidence of her continued distress – with the image of Luke still crisp in her mind's eye in the moments of consciousness between sleep and waking.

She realized Zach had spoken. 'Sorry?'

At last she found the courage to meet Zach's eyes and saw within them an unfathomable depth. A twist of something stirred within her chest as he held her gaze. She knew he hadn't judged her, knew that what had happened to her in Oxford, and in the restaurant in Soufrière, hadn't altered his opinion of her one iota. For all his tetchiness, she experienced a surprisingly strong emotional attachment to Zach.

'So you ran away to London?' he repeated, getting up from the floor and taking a seat next to her on the sofa, his proximity sending spasms of electricity into her fingertips like errant fireworks.

'Yes. It seemed like a good idea at the time,' she whispered.

'Well, if you hadn't, I doubt you would have ended up here in the Caribbean, working for a celebrated chef, visiting tropical rainforests and spectacular waterfalls, discovering new recipes and meeting fabulous people. None of this would have happened if you were still with Luke in Oxford, would it?'

'No.'

'So it's a win-win situation. You got to find out what sort of person you almost ended up marrying as well as expanding your culinary and geographical horizons. Not to mention making some great new friends.'

Zach's mouth was inches away from hers and she daren't move a millimetre. Every nerve ending zinged with excitement and her inner voice screamed, 'Kiss me!' He must have heard, or maybe she had said it out loud, because the next minute his lips were on hers and she tumbled into the most exquisite maelstrom of desire she could remember.

Chapter Seventeen

Millie woke and took a couple of moments to explore her senses. Where was she? Panic ricocheted around her body as the events of the previous evening came screaming back to her – the disastrous date with Marc, her sprint through the rain after being abandoned, the sympathy on Lottie's face, being rescued by a knight in a shiny red Roadster. A spasm of electricity shot through her veins as she remembered exactly where she was, the intimate details of the conversation she'd had with Zach over a rum-laced coffee, and then... Oh, God! The kiss! But was that part of her fuzzy recollections a dream? No way! She could still feel the remnants of the most delicious sensation on her lips and in her heart.

Then a second bolt of alarm hit her. What had happened *after* the kiss? She scrambled around in her brain for an answer, but came up with a complete blank. Her heart fluttered haphazardly with the possibilities until she cracked open her left eye and experienced a huge whoosh of relief – she was still lying on the sofa in his lodge, fully clothed, and covered in a soft fleecy blanket. She inhaled a deep breath and her nostrils filled with the delicious aroma of freshly ground coffee beans and dog-breath. This time she opened her eyes properly to be met by a long pink tongue reaching out towards her nose.

'Euew!'

'Ah, and a good morning to you too, Sleeping Beauty. Coffee?'

'Ah, yes, please.'

Zach handed her a steaming mug of her favourite Blue Mountain coffee and a warm croissant. She devoured her breakfast in seconds, brushing the flakes from her lap to an appreciative Binks.

'Sleep okay?'

'Yes, yes, I did, thank you.'

Heat rushed into her cheeks. She glanced at Zach, but he simply gifted her with his usual cheerful smile accompanied by a side order of mischief.

'Need a lift back to the studio or are you up for joining me and Binks for an early-morning stroll through the grounds? It really is the best time of the day.'

'A walk sounds lovely.'

'Okay. The bathroom's through there. See you outside in a couple of minutes.'

Millie locked the bathroom door and expelled a long sigh. A pendulum of emotions swung through her chest, starting with regret that she hadn't grabbed the opportunity to take things further with Zach. The only explanation was that she had felt so relaxed and content in his company that she had succumbed to the exhaustion caused by the traumatic events of the night and drifted off into a blissful sleep. Oh, God! Had she been snoring?

But did she really want what could only be a brief holiday fling with Zach? Yes, Poppy and Jen would be over the moon to hear that she had taken their advice about moving on. And yes, a no-strings-attached Caribbean romance would certainly help to heal the cracks in her heart, especially with someone as gorgeous as Zach who made her senses zing with pleasure. She could still feel the remnants of the passion their kiss had instilled, like a glowing ember of desire that would take very little to be rekindled. Maybe if they had met at Claudia's UK cookery school branch in the Cotswolds, things could have been different?

However, if she was honest with herself, their blossoming friendship meant so much more to her than a convenient stepping stone towards her recovery from heartbreak and she did not want to risk spoiling what they had achieved. Zach had been the first person outside her family she had opened up to about the way Luke had ended their relationship. She hadn't felt ashamed, or judged, when she had unloaded the burden she had been carrying in her chest like a block of concrete for months. Zach had simply listened, and shared some of his own history, and that had been all it took to make a difference.

She stared at herself in the mirror. She still *looked* like Amelia Harper, with her wild corkscrew curls and the irritating sprinkle of freckles over the bridge of her nose, but she *felt* like a different person; lighter, freer, happier. The whole day stretched ahead of her and she was excited to see where it took her. She jumped into the shower, luxuriating in the warm water, washing away the last vestiges of tiredness and the awkwardness of what had happened last night, both with Marc and her disclosures to Zach about what had happened with Luke. Now that she had told her story once, and had not been ridiculed by her audience, she felt as though she could do it again. The pain was still there, but it had shrunk to a pebble instead of a boulder and a surge of gratitude for Zach's personal brand of sarcasm and wit flooded her veins. Whilst she was in St Lucia, she would trade romance for friendship every time.

She had just finished towel-drying her hair when she heard a sharp bark from outside the window.

'Millie! Millie! We have to go!'

'Okay.'

'Hurry up. We've got to get down to the Parrot. Now!'

The urgency in Zach's voice told her that something was wrong.

'What's happened?' she asked when she saw Zach was already waiting for her in Tim's Roadster.

'Jump in. I'll tell you on the way.'

Within seconds, they were heading down the hill towards Soufrière and Zach was filling her in on a conversation he'd had with Dylan whilst she was in the shower.

'So no one's seen Marc since he left the restaurant last night?'

'No. When he didn't turn up for his morning shift, Lottie tried calling him but he's not answering his mobile,' said Zach. 'She was so angry with him for ditching you that she went storming round to his flat to give him a piece of her mind but there was no sign of him.'

'Maybe the call he got was from a girlfriend and he… erm… he decided to spend the night with her?'

'It's certainly possible, but it's nine o'clock. He should have been at the Purple Parrot for his shift at eight. And something else Dylan said is strange. Apparently when Lottie asked Andrew whether he knew where Marc was he tore into her like a lion denied his lunch, telling her he was Marc's boss not his keeper. Something's going on.'

When they reached the outskirts of the town, Millie remembered that Ella would be arriving at the villa to whip up the very last chocolate-infused recipe on their list before they photographed it and sent it with a celebratory email to Claudia. She left a quick message on her voicemail to let her know she was safe and would catch up with her a little later than expected. She also added an undisguised plea for Ella to appeal to Fitz's slumber-drenched conscience to see if that would speed up the work rate on the kitchen. There were only two days remaining and Millie knew it would take a miracle to finish on time, but she had other things to occupy her mind right now. One trauma at a time!

They arrived at the Purple Parrot and found a parking space in the alleyway that separated the bar from the bicycle-rental shop next door. Instead of using the front door of the bar they jogged around the back. Millie stumbled and tripped over the untied lace of her Sketchers, and Zach shot out an arm to catch her before she fell head first onto the ground. She looked over her shoulder to see that her carelessness had dislodged the lid of a wooden crate crammed with produce.

Millie exchanged a look with Zach. Instead of rubbing her ankle to disperse the pain, she bent forward to investigate further.

'Oh, my God!'

'What?'

'These crates are filled with cocoa pods. What does Andy need two crates of cocoa pods for?'

Zach removed one of the pods. As he lifted it from the box, the pod fell open in his hand. The leathery exterior had been left perfectly intact, but its white fleshy interior had been carefully scraped out to leave just an empty shell.

'Hi, guys. Am I glad to see you!' declared a harassed Lottie. 'Dylan and Ryan have gone up to the Blue Oyster to ask if anyone saw where Marc went after he left Millie stranded there last night.'

'Lottie, what are these doing here?' asked Zach, still staring at the cocoa pod nestled in his palm.

'Oh, Andy uses the liquidized flesh in the Andy's Blast cocktail – delicious! Now let's go. I promised we'd do a sweep of the bars.'

They strode past the colourful shops displaying their wares to the tourists who had begun to emerge from their hiding places, fingering the brightly dyed sarongs, the flimsy beachwear, the carved mahogany masks. But Millie didn't notice any of these retail diversions. A sense of dread had taken up residence in the pit of her stomach and the hackles on the back of her neck cautioned her instincts that something was not how it should be; that Marc hadn't meant to leave her after all and that something awful might have happened to him.

They arrived at Marc's studio flat above a local barber's shop on the outskirts of Soufrière and Lottie's expression reflected Millie's hesitation.

'You know, Dylan's never liked Marc,' Lottie murmured almost to herself, her face pale and pinched.

'What do you mean?' asked Zach.

'Just that he loaned Marc his boat a couple of times over the summer and Marc never returned it when he said he would. And then Dylan found out he was taking the *Nigella* without asking. At night.'

'What? And you didn't think to tell us about this before? Or Millie?'

'Well, I kind of assumed he had been using it to, you know, impress the ladies. To take them on a moonlit sail to some secluded cove, to make love under the stars. You know how it is. Hey, maybe they're still there. Robinson Crusoe-style?' She tried to smile, but Millie could see she was uncomfortable.

Zach hammered on the door. 'Marc!'

The barber meandered to his doorstep and gazed languidly at them, chewing rhythmically on a mouthful of tobacco leaf, his lined face fixed in an expression of contentment.

'Hey, man. Calm the noise. He's not there.'

Zach ignored him and knocked again, but there was no reply. Before Millie and Lottie knew what was happening, he had put his shoulder to the door and given it a sharp shove.

It didn't take them long to search the place and it was true, Marc wasn't there. Whilst every available surface in the bedroom looked like the preparation area for a church jumble sale, it was clear that the bed had not been slept in. He hadn't made it home. However, their brief visit was more than enough time to register a gigantic 3D TV that hung on the wall like a work of art, and a plethora of shiny new high-tech kitchen appliances. It looked as though

Marc had plenty of spare cash to indulge in his love of gadgets. Something didn't add up.

They made their way back to the Purple Parrot in silence, each of them nursing their own fears for Marc's safety. Millie was about to follow Zach and Lottie into the bar when she decided to make a detour and take another look at the cocoa pods in the crates at the back door.

'Hey, where are you going?' called Zach, running to catch up with her.

Millie picked her way carefully down the narrow walkway between the bar and the shack next door, but when she reached the steps all the boxes had vanished. She opened her mouth to express her surprise, but Zach was already sprinting towards the beach. She joined him in the dash, just in time to catch a glimpse of the motorboat chugging around the headland jutting out into the bay to their left. Millie didn't know why, but something told her that the crates were on board. She ran to the water's edge, Zach at her side, and realized it wasn't Marc at the helm as she had suspected, but Andrew.

Chapter Eighteen

Zach and Millie made their way back up the beach, ignoring the curious stares of the sunbathers and the diners enjoying a late breakfast on the veranda of the Purple Parrot. The sound of Zach's mobile ringing prevented Millie from asking for his view on what they had just witnessed.

'Hello?'

Zach stopped in his tracks and found Millie's eyes, the expression on his face the most serious she had seen it. She longed to slip her palm into his, to reacquaint herself with the closeness they had shared the previous night, but until they knew where Marc was, she didn't want to stray into the unchartered territory of exploring where she and Zach went from there.

'Okay, thanks for letting us know, Dylan. Millie and I are on our way to the Parrot. We'll see you there in a few minutes.'

'What? Have they found Marc?'

'Yes. Ryan found him unconscious in a ditch at the side of the road to Castries. He's fine. Ryan wanted to take him to the clinic to get his cuts and bruises checked out, but he refused so he took him to the police station instead where he sang like a canary to Leon. Apparently, he was kidnapped from outside the restaurant last night.'

'Oh, my God! Kidnapped?'

'Yes. Then taken for a drive, knocked on the head and dumped by the roadside.'

'But... but why?'

'I think we just found our mystery cocoa-pod thief.'

'Marc? I thought, well, I thought Andy...'

'I'm going to make a couple of calls. Catch you in a bit.'

They had reached the steps up to the veranda and Zach sauntered towards the street whilst Millie made her way into the Purple Parrot and took a seat on a stool at the bar. Lottie poured her a glass of home-made lemonade before running off to serve a table of Scandinavian tourists whilst Dylan performed the role of temporary bartender. Millie beamed at him, overwhelmingly pleased that the ridiculous scheme had nothing to do with him. As she watched on, Lottie skipped back to the bar to gather her customers' order, and her heart melted when Dylan leaned over to drop a kiss on her friend's forehead. A few minutes later, Zach joined them and downed his drink in one gulp.

'I've just spoken to Leon. The police have intercepted Andy and are escorting him back to the station. After what happened to him last night, Marc's been enthusiastic in his determination to spill the details of Andy's involvement in the drug-smuggling trade.'

'But why ask Marc to steal a few measly cocoa pods? It's crazy.'

'Andy was using cocoa pods to smuggle cocaine. He needed a ready supply, but couldn't risk buying them in the quantities he needed so he began to collect them himself from Claudia's plantation when she wasn't there. A few stray cocoa pods wouldn't be missed. If he was stopped in the jeep, he had a ready excuse about using the flesh in his 'signature' cocktails. If he was intercepted in the dinghy, he'd say he was taking a shipment to a pal in a bar in Martinique to earn a few extra dollars. Who would suspect they were stuffed with cocaine worth thousands of dollars?

'We already know that Andy's business has been slow all season. Everyone is suffering, tourist numbers are down, profits are flat. We know the bank refused him an extension on his loans. And he couldn't sell up and go home, could he? What choice did he have? Anyway, he loves the Purple Parrot and St Lucia. He just needed the money and once he was in, he couldn't get out.'

'And I let Marc borrow my jeep! The scumbag. If I'd known what he was using it for I would never have agreed,' said Dylan, his friendly face creased with anger.

'What about Marc? Why did he get involved?'

'Leon says he's well known to the police in Jamaica. That's why he turned up in St Lucia, to escape their interest. Apparently, they still want to question him.'

'What?' Millie pushed herself up straighter in her seat. 'Oh, my God! I've just remembered. I told Marc about the disappearing cocoa pods last night. That was why he was making that call! It's all my fault.'

'No way is it your fault, Millie,' declared Zach. 'Quite the opposite, in fact. You've actually been instrumental in the arrest of two criminals. Andy did it because he was desperate to save his business. I don't condone what he's done, but I can understand his motivation. Far worse is what Marc did. He's been involved in the drug-trafficking trade for years and, although it pains me to say this, he probably only agreed to a date with you so he could switch on the charm and you would turn a blind eye to his magpie tendencies.'

'Oh, God!' moaned Millie, rubbing her hands over her face.

'I wonder what'll happen to the Purple Parrot?' asked Lottie, fiddling with the friendship bracelet around her wrist as she contemplated the immediate aftermath of Andy's actions. 'I suppose I'll be the new acting manager until we find out. Fancy a job, Millie? Head chef at the Purple Parrot, the best beach bar and restaurant in the whole of Soufrière?'

'Wow, there's an offer!' smirked Zach, reaching out to squeeze Millie's hand before spoiling the gesture by continuing with, 'Shall we tell Lottie about your aversion to culinary orderliness?'

'When is the Paradise Cookery School kitchen due to be finished?' asked Dylan.

'Tomorrow. And before you ask, no, there's no way everything will be completed by then. There's still all the painting to do, the hanging of the artwork, fixing the plinths, the cornices, the door handles, not to mention the cleaning – that will take a whole day at least.'

'But all the heavy-duty stuff is done, right?'

'Well, I suppose so, but even if Fitz and the guys work through the night – which they won't, I've already asked them – it still won't be finished. All the recipes have been triple-tested and approved by Claudia, but without the high-spec facilities the students are expecting, the Chocolate & Confetti course will have to be cancelled.' Millie let out a long, ragged breath of regret. 'Zach's right. I seem to have a habit of attracting chaos and this project is no exception.'

Chapter Nineteen

Millie sipped her breakfast coffee on the veranda overlooking the pool, regretting the fact that she had not indulged in the promised daily swim in its cool, soothing depths. She marvelled once again at the perfection of the view, its verdant beauty a masterpiece framed by palm fronds swaying in the gentle breeze, compared to the nightmare pencil sketch of the kitchen behind her. The early-morning calm was interrupted by the intermittent whizz of an electric drill or the crack of a hammer, punctuated by the occasional squawk of a parrot leaping from the branches of a cocoa tree as Fitz and Alph continued with the mammoth task of finishing the renovations.

She surveyed the kitchen and her heart sank. It was Friday, the day the renovations should have been completed, but it was glaringly obvious there was no way the work would be finished on time. Vic had failed to turn up two mornings in a row and before that she had stumbled upon him in one of the hammocks sleeping off his hangover, snoring like a baby elephant. Fitz and Alph had done their best with one man down, but it wasn't nearly enough.

Nevertheless, the level of workmanship was superb. Fitz was a perfectionist, a true artisan, just not plugged into the same time zone as everyone else. Millie knew you couldn't, and shouldn't, rush quality, but that didn't help when there was a deadline to be met and a group of six chocoholics about to arrive for the Chocolate & Confetti course in three days' time expecting to be coached in the techniques of high-level gastronomy by a prestigious cookery writer in her Caribbean home.

Millie had tried her best to urge Fitz to increase his work rate but with Vic missing in action there was never going to be a sudden spurt of activity. They had also spent most of the morning gossiping about what had happened the previous day at the Purple Parrot until Millie had snapped and asked them to concentrate on the job in hand. However, she had felt so guilty about her uncharacteristic outburst that she had promptly baked a batch of cherry-and-almond scones, delivered them with a cafetière of Jamaica Blue Mountain coffee, and spent a precious hour appeasing them.

Ella had tried to intervene too, explaining to Fitz the importance of adhering to the deadline, even mentioning her friendship with his aunt, but it did not have the desired effect. In fact, the men had just downed tools for their mid-morning break and were reclining in the back of Fitz's white van, drinking the coffee she'd made and taking a snooze.

Millie was about to escape for a shower when she noticed a glint of sunlight against the sink tap, which now, thankfully, had been fitted in the central island unit. However, her eyes had also snagged something else. She approached the marble top of one of the workstations with caution, unable to compute what her brain was telling her.

'Oh, God, no!' she groaned.

A crack ran the whole way across from the corner of the sink to the other side of the work-bench – a distance of fifty centimetres. Not just a crack, a ravine! She slumped onto one of the bar stools, placed her head in her hands and wept. The game was up. No way could they source a new marble countertop by Monday. How could the clients be expected to knead the dough of the hops bread, prepare the peppery paprika cornbread, and mould the coconut rock buns on a damaged surface?

She pulled herself together, dried her eyes and grabbed her phone. It was time to speak to Claudia, to confess that she hadn't been up to the job and to apologize for making such a mess of things. She cringed when she thought of the course being cancelled and a swirl of guilt threatened to over-whelm her, not only towards Claudia but also to the wedding guests whose prenuptial party would be ruined. The call went to voicemail and she left a message for Claudia to phone her back as soon as possible. She had to speak to her before she left for the airport to save her making a wasted journey out to St Lucia, especially with her leg in plaster.

Millie slotted her phone back in her pocket and as she crossed the courtyard she heard the familiar sound of the straining engine of Clavie's taxi ascending the driveway. Ella heaved her bulk from the back seat, but Millie was surprised to see that Lottie was with her, her hair flying high in the breeze, her silver chains jangling around her neck.

'Thanks, Clavie!' Lottie called, slinging her bag over her shoulder and skipping towards Millie to give her a hug. Clavie tooted his horn in response and disappeared back down the hill. 'The Parrot is closed today whilst the police do their thing so I thought maybe you could use an extra pair of hands up here. I'm happy to muck in and do anything you want – especially on the taste-testing side of things.'

'That's really kind of you, Lottie, but I'm not sure it's…'

'I've told Lottie she can help us with the chocolate tiramisu recipe we've been struggling with,' said Ella, making her way towards the studio. 'Today's our last chance to get the recipe perfected, and I think I have an idea that might just work. Come on, the sooner we get started, the sooner we can eat the results!'

The enthusiasm in both Ella and Lottie's faces made Millie feel even worse. She had to come clean with both of them that she was about to inform Claudia she had no option but to cancel the very first Paradise Cookery School course – except she just didn't know how to. Ella was another person to add to the list of people she had failed and a spasm of distress shot through her veins because she knew how much Ella was looking forward to presenting the classes with Claudia and how she was hoping to make this her new career.

'Ah, I just know that the Paradise Cookery School is going to be the best cookery school in the whole of the Caribbean – the recipes that you and Ella have devised are awesome! Claudia'll be booked up until next summer as soon as the reviews go up and she'll be able to open her boutique hotel sooner than she thought, not to mention get the plantation sorted for the tours. I'm going to be the first to put my name on that list – I *lurve* chocolate!'

Ergh, thought Millie, someone else to add to her list. She just couldn't bear it.

'Why don't you both go up to the studio kitchen and I'll be with you in a minute. I just want to talk to Fitz about something.'

She saw Ella's brow crease, but her friend wisely decided to keep her own counsel. Lottie grabbed the numerous carrier bags Clavie had deposited in the courtyard and followed Ella up the stairs to start baking, chatting about how amazing Dylan was and how they planned to manage the Purple Parrot until they knew what was happening with Andrew.

Millie thought her head was going to explode. Her heart thumped in her chest when she rehearsed the enormity of what she had to say to Claudia. She meandered down to the pool terrace and sat under the shade of a lemon tree, her toes tickling the surface of the water, searching her brain for a solution that wouldn't mean disappointing so many people. She checked her phone to see if Claudia had called her back as she hadn't heard it ring, but there was nothing.

'What's up? Has Messy Millie been banished from the kitchen?'

Millie couldn't be bothered to rise to the task of challenging Zach over his name-calling. She knew how much he wanted to arrange activities for the cookery-school attendees, and how upset he was going to be when she confessed how she had failed, but she needed to confide in someone or she would be looking her sanity in the rear-view mirror.

'The first Paradise Cookery School course is being cancelled,' said Millie, her throat tightening against the words.

'What? Why? I thought you and Ella had every-thing planned? Every recipe triple- and quadruple-tested, every detail ironed out, every ingredient sourced and ready to be delivered for Monday. Ella told me that you've even got a whole host of backup recipes just in case some of the ingredients aren't available...'

'It's not the culinary side of things,' said Millie, lowering her voice and tossing a look over her shoulder to the veranda where Alph was smoking a cigarette and contemplating an unopened tin of white emulsion as if he had never seen one before in his life.

'What is it then?'

'Well, as you can see, there's no way everything will be ready in time to receive paying guests. We've lost Vic for some reason that's not entirely clear, and the kitchen needs to pass certain standards for health-and-safety reasons. Claudia would never run a course bearing her name that posed a potential risk to a guest's well-being.'

Unexpectedly, Millie was ambushed by a burst of sobbing. All the stress of what had happened the previous day, coupled with the delays she'd fought so hard to keep on top of, and the discovery of the crack in the countertop, was suddenly all too much. Zach sat down beside her, waiting until her tears ceased and she turned to meet his gaze. He smiled and reached out to tuck a loose curl behind her ear, a gesture that sent a sparkle of attraction through Millie.

'You know, Millie, this isn't your fault. When Fitz was hired to do the kitchen renovations he told Claudia that three weeks was the absolute minimum he needed to complete the work to the standard she required. He was ready to start on time, but as you know, Claudia had her riding accident and there was a week's delay. It was always going to be a tight timescale to get everything done. Claudia knew that, but of course her mind was on other things, and who can blame her.'

Millie stared at Zach. What he had said was true, but it didn't make her feel any better. She had wanted the project to be a success so much. For her own peace of mind, she needed to know that she was still capable of delivering results, and had dared to hope that her sojourn in St Lucia would help her to turn the corner on her crisis of confidence, not only emotionally but professionally. She had even started to toy with the idea of looking for a head chef's position when she got back home.

'Thanks, Zach.'

Zach produced a pristine cotton handkerchief from the pocket of his shorts and handed it to her.

'Now, you might be lots of things, Amelia Harper, but you don't strike me as a quitter, so let's take a look at the kitchen and see what's left to be done before we throw the towel in the pool! Not everyone is going to let you down, you know. You have lots of friends here who will be only too pleased to offer you their services in return for a cold beer and one of your chocolate brownies!' Zach sprang to his feet, leaving behind a delicious tang of citrussy cologne. 'Come on, show me the plans.'

Millie followed him, surreptitiously storing his damp handkerchief in her pocket, not wanting Fitz to know she had been about to call it a day and tell him to go home. She unearthed the torn and paint-splattered plans from beneath a pile of vivid artwork, and together she and Zach scrutinized every aspect of the renovations, before cross-examining Fitz on what there was left to do. Millie scribbled everything on a notepad, making a list of the outstanding tasks as Alph looked on with an expression of scepticism and not a little trepidation.

Next, Zach disappeared into the courtyard where he paced backwards and forwards, his phone clenched to his ear, snippets of animated conversation floating through the air.

'Great! Thanks, Anisha, and round up Travis too, will you?' And, 'Yes, Dylan, Lottie is here. She and Ella are on cooking duties. It'll be the best barbeque you've had all year, I promise! And tell Ryan the beers are on me.'

Zach slotted his phone back into his pocket and strode back to the veranda.

'Okay, Millie. Prepare yourself to be amazed. You are about to experience what can be achieved when a bunch of friends pull together to help another friend out. Now, I don't want to hear one more word about cancelling the course next week. Why don't you spend the next hour prioritizing the remaining jobs so that when the cavalry arrives you can set them to work straight away?'

An upsurge of gratitude grabbed her unawares and, despite their slight awkwardness since she had spent the night crashed out on his sofa at the lodge, she flung herself at Zach, hugging him to her, only just managing to grip on to her emotions by her fingertips. To her surprise and delight, he picked her up and spun her around, depositing a kiss on her cheek when he set her back down. It wasn't a patch on the embrace they had shared on Wednesday night, but the connection still sent waves of desire running through her veins. She briefly wondered what would happen if she wasn't leaving for the UK on Sunday.

However, there was too much to do to dwell on what ifs. Millie spent the next hour going through her list with a pencil behind her ear, a tape measure around her wrist, making detailed notes and issuing instructions. Fitz and Alph scampered around like lambs under her firm but friendly direction, making their own contributions and suggestions for improvements.

Ella and Lottie appeared an hour later with a platter of fried-fish-and-mango-chutney sandwiches and a pitcher of freshly squeezed lemonade.

'I've spoken to Henri,' said Ella, her multi-coloured bangles tinkling at her wrist as she poured out their drinks. 'He's just finishing a piece on illegal rum production for the weekend issue of the *Tribune* and he's promised to present himself for inspection on the drill line first thing tomorrow morning. Leon doesn't think he can get away from work, but has offered his services on Saturday night and Sunday. I've also left a message for my brother Byron and I'm sure he'll be delighted to be roped in for a bit of painting.'

'He will if he wants to taste my cookies!' exclaimed Lottie.

At six o'clock, Ella and Lottie discarded their Paradise Cookery School aprons and squeezed into Henri's little Fiat for the journey back to Soufrière.

'I'm so happy that you're about to experience how the St Lucian community can pull together and make good things happen,' smiled Henri as he stowed his mother's oversized bag in the boot and gave Millie a farewell hug. 'See you tomorrow, bright and early.'

Millie saw that Ella had tears in her eyes. She watched her friend extract a delicate lace handker- chief from her sleeve and dab them away, whilst she swallowed down her own. She truly felt as though she was part of an extended Caribbean family and a curl of regret that her visit was so short-lived wriggled through her stomach.

'Thanks, Henri. Ella, Lottie, see you tomorrow.'

Millie watched the car trundle away down the hill and disappear around the bend. She went in search of Zach but couldn't find him so she retreated to her studio above the garage for a good cry. The release was satisfying and afterwards, she fell into an untroubled sleep until she was woken by a knock on her front door.

'Miss Millie?'

Dusk had started to ripple over the horizon, spreading a wave of cerise and pink over the distant sea as she dashed down the stairs to meet Fitz and Alph who were busy loading up the van for the day.

'We'll be off now, but we'll be back for the seven-thirty roll call.'

'Erm, I think it's seven,' said Millie with a grin, knowing that he was trying it on. 'You are still in charge of operations, Fitz, but now you will have ten more willing workers under your direction, all looking to you for leadership. What will we all do if you're not here to crack the whip?'

Millie watched as Fitz straightened his spine and shoved back his shoulders. 'Seven a.m. on the dot, it is. See you then.'

Millie smiled and waved as he jumped into the cab of his dilapidated white van next to Alph and reversed down the driveway to the road, their favourite reggae music blasting forth. A feeling of pride invaded her chest. She had never had the confidence to speak to Fitz in that way before. Yet when she had done so he had responded with enthusiasm, with pleasure even, at the authority and responsibility she had bestowed upon his shoulders. Maybe if she had been able to do that from the start they wouldn't be facing the uphill challenge that was ahead of them now.

Another lesson in life for her to dwell on.

Millie slumped down on one of the sunloungers and took stock of the last few hours. If all the offers of help materialized, she had every confidence that the kitchen would be finished by the time Claudia arrived on Sunday afternoon. That would give her and Ella a few hours to talk through the culinary side of things and the Paradise Cookery School *would* go ahead on Monday morning as scheduled. The Chocolate & Confetti course *would* be a tremendous success and Ella would get her coveted job as a guest presenter and Zach would be able to continue with his plans for extracurricular activities which he could proudly pass on to Jake when his stay in the Caribbean came to an end.

She pushed herself up and slotted her feet into her sparkly flip-flops. It was time she went to the lodge to thank Zach for everything he had done to save the day.

Chapter Twenty

Despite Millie's last-minute doubts, all three tradesmen turned up the following day at seven a.m. just minutes before Henri, Ella and her brother Byron, and Travis and Anisha, who had negotiated a rare day off to be part of the team. Dylan and Lottie floated in with Ryan and a friend of theirs, Connor, at seven-thirty. The couple were bug-eyed from lack of sleep, having spent the night celebrating their new relationship. Lottie reported that although she had wanted to keep the Purple Parrot open, Leon had requested that it remain closed until the following weekend at least to allow their investigations to take place.

Before she had retired to bed the previous night, Millie had tried to call Claudia again. She knew she was due to arrive the following day, but she still needed to speak to her and couldn't understand why her calls kept going to voicemail. However, she *had* enjoyed a long chat with Poppy who had suggested that she should consider asking Étienne for a week's unpaid leave so she could take advantage of being part of the very first of Claudia Croft's Paradise Cookery School courses, as the experience would be invaluable for any future dreams she harboured of sharing her own knowledge with a group of students.

Millie had brushed her friend's suggestion aside, keen to return home to normality, eager to indulge in an extended session of gossip. Poppy had casually dropped into the conversation that her date with the guy at the Italian deli across the road hadn't worked out, but that she now had set her sights on a tall, dark, handsome chef from the bistro at the end of the street. They had already been out on a couple of dates and she couldn't wait to introduce Millie to his friend, Charles.

For some reason, Millie did not reciprocate by sharing with Poppy her feelings for Zach as she couldn't put them into words. Yes, they had shared a stomach-churning kiss that night in his lodge, and yes, being with him sent her emotions haywire, but she was leaving the next day, so there was no point in pursuing their connection any further, even if Zach had shown such an inclination – which he hadn't. However, she had a great deal to thank Zach for, not least the fact that talking to him about what had happened with Luke had put the whole episode into perspective and she hadn't thought of her ex-fiancé once since their conversation.

Why couldn't she have met Zach earlier? But she knew she might not have appreciated his unique brand of down-to-earth advice if it had been presented before she was ready.

Nevertheless, a part of her did wish she could stay in St Lucia, to spend more than just an hour with Claudia, to take part in the Chocolate & Confetti course, to see where her friendship with Zach would take her. And she had to admit that Zach wasn't the only person she would miss when she went home. She couldn't get her head around the fact that she would never see Ella again, especially when the Caribbean chef had told her the previous day that she was like the daughter she had never had. But before she could stroll too far down her life's highway of regrets, Millie was called upon for her advice.

'Hey, Millie, where do you want this canvas hung?'

'Shall I finish the gloss work in the porch?'

'Where are the handles for the drawers?'

'Who's supposed to be washing the windows?'

The villa had taken on a buzz of frenetic activity. They drilled, hammered, sawed, polished, painted and cleaned, all under Millie's subtle direction, although she was careful to defer to Fitz on all of the major decisions – but everyone knew who was really in charge. Fitz even managed to repair the crack in the worktop with some magic adhesive which when polished, looked like a natural flaw in the marble.

When dusk finally arrived, the gang congregated on the veranda, devouring Ella's freshly baked chicken stuffed with figs and apricots, nervously sipping at their coffee and mango juice, as Millie and Ella toured the kitchen double-checking every detail against their lists.

Every surface was scrutinized. Stray finger marks were wiped from the tiles and the stainless-steel appliances. Sawdust was banished from the cornices and the copper pans. Millie tested the flow of the hot and cold water from every tap, ignited each of the gas burners one by one, and tried the sockets with a hand-held blender, before finally declaring herself satisfied and dispatching Vic to collect the furniture from storage.

There was a last push to stage the plump white sofas at a satisfactory angle and dress the lamp and coffee tables with the floral displays donated by Denise. Lottie cleaned off a speck of glue from the front of the refrigerator, Dylan fixed the spotlights so they were at precisely the right angle for each of the workstations and Anisha affixed a strand of Caribbean-themed bunting around the French doors.

The Paradise Cookery School was finished!

'Thank you, everyone,' said Millie, ignoring the tears streaming down her cheeks unchecked. 'If it wasn't for every single one of you offering your help today, the kitchen would never have been finished on time. You are an absolutely awesome team and to show my appreciation, and to say goodbye, I'm throwing a party here tomorrow afternoon for when Claudia arrives from the airport. The drinks will be mixed by our brand-new bar and restaurant manager, Miss Lottie Bedford, ably assisted by her sidekick, Travis Scott!'

Henri, Dylan and Ryan slapped Travis on the back and exchanged congratulatory fist bumps. The young artist lowered his lashes in a shy smile of acknowledgement. It had taken a great deal of persuasion by Lottie and Anisha to peel him away from his artwork, but he had agreed to help Lottie in the Purple Parrot until she found a replacement for Marc and Andrew was informed what his future held. It meant extra cash for Travis, which he could definitely do with, and Lottie still had her job and could meet her rent, not that she was going anywhere.

'Claudia is going to be delighted with the way the villa is looking. I can feel it in my bones,' declared Ella as they strolled out to the veranda. 'I can't wait to get started with the cookery-school tutorials. I don't think I've been this excited since I was a teenager.'

'Okay, okay, ladies, or should I say slave-drivers?' said Ryan. 'We're all desperate for a shower and a beer and a rest from all this hard work. See you tomorrow!'

Everyone made their way to the courtyard, laughing and joking, teasing Lottie and Dylan as they exchanged a kiss before jumping into separate jeeps. A wave of intense happiness swept through Millie. She had not known a single person in St Lucia when she arrived two weeks ago, soaking wet, jet-lagged and alone. Now she could count on ten new friends, people who had come to the aid of a stranger in more ways than one, who had worked until their knuckles bled and their backs ached, all for the prize of friendship, a belly full of great food and the occasional bottle of Red Stripe.

Marc was wrong – it wasn't money that talked; it was friendship.

Chapter Twenty-One

Everything was set for Claudia's arrival. Lottie had helped to hang a necklace of fairy lights over the doors and windows and around the balustrade overlooking the terrace. The infinity pool's underwater lights shone so brightly that the water glowed with azure-tinged splendour and was the focal point of that afternoon's gathering. Cathedral candles of varying heights flickered inside storm lanterns dotted around the decking and the table groaned under an abundance of treats all provided by Ella and Denise who had worked all morning in the brand-new kitchen. It had been a huge relief to Millie that every appliance had worked the way it should. It was the best day she'd had in the Caribbean – freed from the stress of delivering the kitchen project on time.

Everyone had turned up for the celebration – and to wish Millie a safe journey home and good luck in her future ventures. Zach had been curiously taciturn all morning and whenever she caught his eye to offer him a smile, he turned away to speak to whoever was standing next to him. Binks snoozed happily at his feet, but with one eye peeled for discarded titbits.

Millie still hadn't heard from Claudia. She had asked Ella to call her at her house in the Cotswolds that morning, but there was no reply. They had checked Claudia's last email for the precise details of her flight, searched the internet to make sure that the plane had left on time, and dispatched Clavie to collect her from the airport. Despite the glorious success of the kitchen, a curl of trepidation still nestled in Millie's stomach, along with a buzz of excitement at Claudia's imminent arrival.

Whilst Dylan and Lottie happily exchanged kisses under the palm trees in the garden, Ryan, Connor and Travis pushed each other in the hammocks like toddlers in a playground. Henri and Alisha were chatting at the cocktail table, Henri animated in his explanation of how he was sure his investigative journalism for the *Tribune* would force those in authority to take a closer interest in the youth-unemployment problem that was gripping their community.

It was only a matter of minutes before Clavie was due to show up with Claudia in his clapped-out old taxi and she would get her first glimpse of her exciting new enterprise. A spasm of nerves shot down Millie's spine, but then she relaxed. How could Claudia not adore the clean white lines of the walls and the floor tiles, the elegant sleekness of the Italian marble and the shining stainless steel of the appliances? Everything was perfect, including Travis's artwork, which lent a colourful splash of the true spirit of the Caribbean amongst the minimalism.

The kitchen was ready to receive its first Paradise Cookery School students on Monday morning – less than eighteen hours away. Millie was proud of what had been achieved and felt a stab of disappointment that she would not be there to witness their enjoyment and to hear their exclamations of amazement at the beauty both inside the villa and in the surrounding tropical landscape. She knew the menus they had devised over the last two weeks showcased the very best that Caribbean culinary culture had to offer the discerning foodie. She was also confident that there would be no question whatsoever that the Chocolate & Confetti course would be the first in long line of tailor-made tutorials and that the hotly anticipated *Claudia Croft Caribbean Cookery* book would fly from the shelves when it was published next year.

Millie checked her grandmother's silver Tiffany watch for what seemed like the hundredth time. Four-thirty. She leaned over the rail of the veranda, her toes leaving the decking, to glance down the driveway, but she couldn't see any sign of Clavie's taxi or hear the engine straining to mount the incline. Trust him to be late! She scrolled through the Arrivals schedule on her phone and saw that the British Airways flight had landed on time.

'Hey, Millie, any news from Claudia? She should be here by now.' Henri draped his arm over her shoulder and she was rewarded with a whiff of his spicy eau de cologne. 'Did I tell you the *Daily Telegraph* in the UK have agreed to run my article on the increase in the use of the old drug routes through the Caribbean in their Sunday supplement?' he asked, his expression modest, almost nonchalant.

'Wow, that's fabulous news!' Millie hugged her friend. 'Congratulations!'

'They also want to commission a professional photographer and I need to tweak a few paragraphs for them, but it's a great honour. And I've been approached by *Le Figaro* too. If I'm stuck on the translation, I can always ask you to help out, eh?'

'Of course! I'm so happy for you, Henri.'

Henri simply smiled and helped himself to a dish of his mother's mango sorbet topped with freshly frozen mint leaves.

Millie glanced at her watch again. Four forty-five p.m.

She decided to seek out Zach and ask him why he was ignoring her. She would be leaving for the airport in less than an hour and she didn't want to go without understanding the reason he was distancing himself from her. She had taken just two steps towards the courtyard where he was chatting to Dylan when Lottie intercepted her mission, glancing at Zach and then Millie.

'I've told Zach he's being ridiculous, but I think it's a kind of protective mechanism.'

'What do you mean?'

'We've all noticed that Zach's been avoiding you. Dylan challenged him and all he would say is that he wishes he was catching the plane back to the UK with you. He won't admit it, but he's going to miss you, Millie. You two have become firm friends, but maybe it's a little more than that?"

Millie opened her mouth to answer, but her phone buzzed in the pocket of her glamorous black jumpsuit. She saw Claudia's number flash onto the screen and her body flooded with relief.

'Hi, Claudia. How was your flight?'

The line was faint and crackly and she could barely make out what Claudia was saying. She dashed from the veranda into the courtyard, her hand cupped over her ear, concentrating hard on deciphering the words.

'I'm so sorry, Millie… Taken back into hospital yesterday… Complications… Doctors refuse to allow me to travel…'

'Oh, Claudia, are you okay?'

'So sorry… and I can't present the Chocolate & Confetti course tomorrow…'

'But… but you have to be here!' Millie blurted, fireworks of panic going off in her head.

Millie thought of all the hard work and the sacrifices her friends had made to pull off the triumph of the year and it now looked as though the Paradise Cookery School would be cancelled despite it all. Her throat tightened around a lump the size of a golf ball but she swallowed down her disappointment. It was clear that Claudia felt far worse.

'Tim has sent you an email… Can't cancel… The guests have already arrived in St Lucia for the wedding… Taken the liberty…'

'Claudia? I can't hear you! Claudia!'

'What's going on?' asked Zach, appearing at her side, his forehead creased in a mixture of concern and confusion. 'Was that Claudia?'

'Yes. She's been taken back into hospital. That's why I haven't been able to get hold of her for the last couple of days. Obviously she can't fly.'

'So what's happening about the cookery course tomorrow?'

'I don't know. Apparently Tim's sent me an email.'

Millie scrolled through her inbox for the missive, her heart pounding painfully. She scanned the words swiftly, before raising her eyes to meet Zach's, her mouth gaping.

'What? What does it say?'

Mutely, Millie handed her phone over to Zach.

'Yes! Fantastic!' and before Millie knew what he was doing, Zach had grabbed her around the waist and swung her round and round until her feet lifted from the ground and she yelled at him to put her down. 'It means you get to stay!'

'But I don't know the first thing about presenting a cookery course!'

'You didn't know anything about supervising kitchen renovations until last week, but you've done an awesome job – with a little help from your friends.'

'Zach...'

'Ella is a superb chef and a whirlwind of energy and creativity when it comes to culinary crises. She'll support you. You have the professional expertise and the credentials. Perhaps you could play up your Michelin star?'

'But what if the guests complain about not getting Claudia?'

'Well, if her promise of a complete set of her cookery books, personalized and autographed for each of them, isn't enough, then I think the fact that she's offered to reimburse them every penny if they're not happy will do the trick!'

Belatedly, Millie noticed the about-turn in Zach's mood from the cold shoulder he had been giving her earlier. Could it really be because she was staying on in St Lucia? Did that mean that Lottie was right and…

'But I can't stay here. Étienne…'

'Read the last paragraph again.' Zach handed Millie's phone back to her

'Tim's offered him an all-expenses-paid trip to the villa in return for giving me a week's unpaid leave from the café?'

'And promised to pay you an enhanced fee for co-presenting the course, as well as your normal salary. Can't say fairer than that,' said Zach, his dark eyes alight.

'It's not the money I'm bothered about. It's the fact that I will be presenting a bespoke culinary experience to six strangers who are expecting the acclaimed Claudia Croft, cookery writer extraordinaire. I can't do it, not by myself!'

'You'll be with Ella.'

'Oh, Zach, I'm not sure…'

'Haven't we talked about this? Before you can fly off to new beginnings, you first have to jump! Jump, Millie! Show the world what you're capable of. Don't let yourself be defined by one unfortunate incident months ago. I know you can do this. I know you'll be sensational, especially when you have a secret weapon up your sleeve.'

'Secret weapon? What secret weapon?'

Millie saw Zach's face soften as he took a step closer to her and reached for her hand, pulling her towards him so that his breath tickled her cheek. His proximity ignited flames of such intense desire in her stomach that her breath was whipped from her lungs. Seconds later, his lips were on hers and Millie experienced a rush of exhilaration, a feeling of deep joy that she was where she was supposed to be. Zach broke away far too soon and dragged her towards where the party was still in full flow.

'Come on, Magnificent Millie. You've got to tell Ella the good news! Then I suggest we get rid of this lot and spend some time alone… planning your daily presentations?'

There was that mischievous smirk Millie had grown used to. She couldn't wait to take him up on his offer, but she knew she had to speak to Ella first. She found her chatting away about a new recipe with Denise and Lottie.

'Millie, where have you been? And I'm getting quite worried about Claudia.'

'Claudia is fine… well, actually, can I have a quick word?'

Millie guided Ella into the villa's living area where they fell onto one of the white sofas, sinking into its plush depths.

'Claudia's not coming.'

She watched Ella's eyes widened in confusion. 'Why ever not?'

Millie explained the situation in as few words as possible and was thrilled at Ella's positive reaction. 'You will be marvellous, my dear. It'll be an honour to work beside you. We will do it together. Haven't we just spent the last two weeks training for this? I will come every day to prepare the ingredients and we can share the role of presenter.'

'Thank you, Ella, but we'll need someone else to help us. Someone who knows the way around a kitchen, who can slot effortlessly…'

'Me! I'll help.' Lottie stood at the door, having eavesdropped on everything Millie had said. 'The

Purple Parrot doesn't open until the Chocolate & Confetti course is over. It's perfect timing!'

The young girl's pretty face lit with resplendent enthusiasm and Millie's heart squeezed. She glanced at Ella who gave a nod of affirmation and the three women hugged each other, tears flowing freely, until a voice interrupted their celebrations.

'Hello? Hello? Oh, I'm sorry to intrude. Is this the Paradise Cookery School? I'm looking for Claudia Croft? I'm Imogen Spencer. My friends and I are booked on the Chocolate & Confetti cookery course tomorrow. I'm just checking that everything is okay? Ooooh, I'm so excited. It's going to be the perfect pre-wedding treat. Are they cocoa trees outside?'

Acknowledgements

I loved writing and researching the Paradise Cookery School series, spending every day in the glorious (virtual) Caribbean sunshine was amazing. However, the story would not have sparkled without the magic touch of my fabulous editor at Canelo, Louise Cullen, to whom I say a massive thank you.

The Paradise Cookery School

Sunshine & Secrets
Confetti & Confusion
Mistletoe & Mystery

Read on for an exclusive preview
of another novel in
The Paradise Cookery School series

Confetti & Confusion

Chapter One

'Hello, everyone, and welcome to Claudia Croft's Paradise Cookery School here on the gorgeous island of St Lucia. I'm Amelia Harper and this week, along with my co-presenter, Ella Johnson, I'll be demonstrating a whole host of delicious recipes before giving you all the opportunity to try them out for yourselves under our supervision.'

Millie inhaled a deep breath to steady her rampaging nerves, but her heart continued to hammer out a symphony of fear, sending spasms of electricity out to her fingertips. How had she got herself into this? Overseeing the kitchen renovations for celebrity cookery book writer and chef Claudia Croft was one thing, but presenting one of her prestigious courses was quite another. As she stared out at the eager faces in front of her she pulled herself together. What was she so worried about? She could do this!

'At the request of Imogen, our fabulous bride-to-be, Claudia has designed a week of personalised tutorials that she's called Chocolate and Confetti, crammed with mouth-watering chocolate-inspired recipes, all of which you'll be able to taste-test at the end of each day.'

'Yay!' squealed Gracie, the youngest member of the pre-wedding hen party at eight years old, clapping her hands and pogoing up and down on the spot in her two-sizes-too-big-for-her apron. A wave of laughter rippled around the room as Imogen patted her niece's blonde curls affectionately.

'Also, as a special treat, a good friend of ours, Lottie Bedford, has designed a range of delicious cocktails made from locally sourced ingredients, including a really delicious recipe that contains the flesh of the cocoa pods you see growing in the villa's grounds.'

'Mmm!'

This time the sigh of pleasure came from the adult members of the group, particularly Imogen's sister, Karen, and her bridesmaids, Carla and Harriet, whilst her mother, Julia, rolled her eyes at them.

'Don't worry, there'll be a few alcohol-free versions to choose from, too. Lottie really is a maestro at mixing exotic flavours. Ella and I had hoped that she would be with us this week but she's been promoted to manager of the Purple Parrot bar in Soufrière after the proprietor had a run-in with the local police. So, shaking cocktails will be a new skill that we can learn together.'

Millie glanced around at the six chocoholics who had chosen to spend the week before Imogen's glamourous nuptials learning how to create all things cocoa-related instead of indulging in the more traditional exploits of raucous hen parties down in the bars and restaurants in Soufrière, the former St Lucian capital at the bottom of the hill. Not only would they be turning their hands to producing desserts, cakes and patisserie containing their beloved bean, but Millie also intended to explain how the chocolate they were using was produced from the tiny nibs found inside the weird purple-brown pods that grew on the trees in the villa's extensive grounds.

'So, I hope you all have a fun and productive week but that you also leave the Paradise Cookery School with a treasure trove of new recipes in your repertoire with which to impress your friends when you return home.'

'If you can teach Imogen to bake anything that isn't tinged with the aroma of burnt tyres, or completely caramelised to a crisp, then I'll be happy!' laughed Julia, smirking at her daughter, her affection apparent for all to see.

'Hey! Is it my fault that I prefer to support the products made by our friends at Patisserie Valerie and Hotel Chocolat?' Imogen retaliated, a wide grin splitting her cheeks.

'Okay, so I thought I would start by demonstrating a couple of my favourite childhood recipes passed down from my French grandmother – chocolate truffle tortes with hazelnut brittle and chocolate and cherry madeleines.'

Millie smoothed her trembling palms over the front of the pale-lemon apron that had been embroidered with Claudia's famous CC logo. Her knees shook a little and she was grateful she'd had the good sense to ditch her heels for a pair of sequinned flip-flops. However, as soon as she began to weigh out the ingredients, her anxiety vanished and the next three hours passed in a whirl of frenzied activity. She even had to admit that she was enjoying herself; after all, baking had always been her go-to activity to escape the grenades that life had thrown in her path.

When Claudia had asked her to step into her shoes at the last minute, Millie's first reaction had been to panic. She had been more than happy to temporarily swap her job as a pastry chef in a tiny patisserie in London to oversee the upgrade of the villa's kitchen after Claudia broke her leg in a horse riding accident. It had been the perfect opportunity to escape the heartache caused by the breakdown of her relationship with Luke and spend some time in the Caribbean sunshine. However, she had never in her wildest dreams thought she would still be there two weeks later, wearing the course presenter badge!

So, here she was, standing in front of six well-heeled women – in both senses of the word – all of whom were expecting to be guided through the labyrinth of culinary excellence by the celebrated TV chef and cookery writer. She had tried to refuse, but by the time Claudia's doctors had forbidden her to travel, the hen party guests had already arrived at the luxury boutique hotel where the wedding of the year was taking place at the end of the week, and it was too late to cancel. Millie didn't want to let Claudia down – or to disappoint the bridal party – so, against her better judgment, she had reluctantly agreed to step into the breach.

As the proud owner of a Michelin star, she *did* have the necessary culinary qualifications to deliver the course, and she and Ella *had* spent the previous two weeks triple-testing every single recipe on the itinerary. Even so, she was terrified that Claudia's very first Chocolate & Confetti course would be a flop, that the Paradise Cookery School would receive dreadful reviews, which in turn would jeopardise any plans Claudia had for future courses. Whilst that scenario would be upsetting for Claudia, who adored her Caribbean home, because her main place of business was located in a manor house in the Cotswolds, it wouldn't affect her business too much. What Millie was most concerned about was how the failure would affect Ella, her co-host and newfound friend, whose long-held dream to run a cookery school was about to come true. Everything rested on Millie and she had to give it her best shot.

At lunchtime, the group broke from their activities to gather on the veranda and feast on a kaleidoscope of Caribbean-inspired salads prepared by Ella before resuming their positions behind their respective workstations for the afternoon tutorial.

'I'll now pass the culinary baton over to Ella, who is going to demonstrate how to make mini chocolate-orange roulades filled with marmalade made from the oranges that are grown right here on the Croft estate. Then, to end the day with a sizzle, we'll make one of Ella's signature recipes that her son, Henri, swears are the best he's ever tasted – chilli-chocolate brownies.'

'Yay!' squealed Gracie. 'I love chocolate brownies!'

'You might want to add a little less chilli to your own recipe!' laughed Ella, taking Millie's place at the marble-topped demonstration bench, every inch the Caribbean cook extraordinaire.

That day, in honour of the occasion, Ella's ample proportions were enhanced by a tropically inspired kaftan scattered with sequin and gemstone embellishments, and a necklace made of hand-crafted wooden beads the size of quail's eggs with matching earrings. Millie smiled; her co-presenter clearly lived by the mantra that excess was better when it came to technicoloured wardrobe choices.

Listening to Ella's melodic Caribbean lilt as she explained the importance of lightness of touch when it came to making sponge cake, Millie's heart gave a squeeze of gratitude for her friend's expertise and calm professionalism in contrast to her own tendency towards culinary clutter. She adored Ella – with her penchant for exotic spices and habit of dispensing blunt, yet level-headed advice. Her knowledge of Caribbean cookery was extensive, embroidered over the years with a variety of influences from Creole to French, from Spanish to American. Millie knew she couldn't have done any of this without her support.

'Take care when slicing the oranges,' cautioned Ella.

'Yes, Immie darling, we don't want the bride trussed up in bandages on her wedding day, do we? Not exactly the must-have accessory for the theme I have planned for the wedding,' said Julia, who had reluctantly swapped her Italian-designed cropped jacket for one of Claudia's signature pale-lemon aprons. With her towering Louboutins, her whole ensemble screamed the sartorial equivalent of 'look at me!' Yet her intensely groomed caramel bob had already succumbed to the ambient humidity, and her early morning visit to the hotel's hairdressers had turned out to be a pointless exercise. 'Never mind spoiling the photographs!'

'Oh, Mum! I wish you'd relax over the whole "attention-to-detail" thing you have going on. We're supposed to be enjoying ourselves, not stressing over the wedding arrangements. We have a wedding planner to do all that.'

'But she's useless. She was over an hour late for our appointment yesterday morning and when she did eventually turn up she'd forgotten to bring the floral samples with her. And would you believe that when I asked about the butterflies she looked at me as though I was crazy. I bet she hasn't even ordered them. Honestly, Imogen, I don't know what we are paying her for...'

'Mum, I keep telling you, Alex and I just want a laid-back wedding day, surrounded by the people we love in a relaxed and stress-free atmosphere. I definitely won't be devastated if we don't get to release a kaleidoscope of butterflies after we've exchanged our vows, or if the confetti doesn't have our picture on it. In fact, why can't we have rice? That's what I wanted in the first place.'

'That's what peasants do at weddings!' shot back Julia, combing her fingers through her straw-like hair.

'No it's not,' laughed Imogen, tossing jagged lumps of orange peel into the jam pan that was on the hob she shared with her mother, whose own fruit segments were perfectly sliced. 'I really don't understand why we couldn't have had a quiet country wedding at home. I loved the idea of the village fête theme Karen suggested.' Imogen smiled at her sister, who was concentrating on showing Gracie how to grate her chocolate without also grating her fingers. 'Hoopla, juggling, guess how many sweets in the jar, a huge meringue-like marquee, pastel bunting floating in the breeze. I think our friends would have loved that!'

'Don't be facetious, dear. It doesn't suit you.'

Millie left the bride's family to their obviously well-rehearsed argument and moved on to the adjacent marble-topped workstation where Imogen's two bridesmaids were attempting a version of Ella's chilli-chocolate brownie recipe. A giggle, followed by a very unladylike snort of laughter, erupted from Carla as she tried to conceal the fact that her cheeks were bulging like an over-zealous hamster, obviously having started early on the taste-testing part of the day. Not to be outdone, Harriet was squirting chocolate buttercream into her mouth from a piping bag. Every spare inch of their countertop was scattered with culinary debris — splodges of butter, snail trails of powdered sugar and dots of melted chocolate, not to mention the jumble of discarded implements in the sink.

Millie smiled. She was the last person to chastise anyone for making a mess in the kitchen, having been told on more than one occasion that she could bring chaos to an empty room by many a friend and colleague, and more recently by Zach Barker.

Her spirits edged up a notch further when she thought of Claudia and Tim Croft's prickly estate manager whom she had crossed spatulas with when she arrived at the villa two weeks ago. From a difficult start, when she had mistakenly thought Zach was the gardener rather than their highly qualified estate manager on secondment from their country manor house in the UK, they had gone on to form an unexpected friendship. In the space of a few days, he had achieved what her friend Poppy back home in London had failed to do in six months – forced her to put her disastrous relationship history into perspective.

So what if Luke had ditched her at their engagement party, in front of all their friends and family, and run off into the sunset with her best friend's mother? That was his decision and there was nothing she could do about it. No amount of tears and painful soul-searching would change the situation, or lessen the embarrassment. With his special brand of sarcastic wit, Zach had helped her to face the demons that had taken up residence in her mind and serve them with an eviction notice. They hadn't left yet, but they had packed their bags and ordered a taxi. She was even starting to come to terms with the fact that Luke and Donna were expecting their first child in a few months' time.

Satisfied that Carla and Harriet had everything under control, Millie sauntered back to the demonstration bench. She allowed her thoughts to linger briefly on the previous day when she and Zach had shared a kiss beneath the palm trees and a pleasurable swirl of desire meandered through her veins. However, mingled with the undoubted pull of attraction was a nugget of uncertainty. Did she really want a holiday fling? Even if it was with someone who made every one of her senses zing with excitement and anticipation whenever they were together? Because, sadly, that was all it could be – at the end of her brief sojourn in paradise, she would return to her life in London and it was unlikely they would see each other again.

An enticing fragrance of warm sugar and chocolatey sponge cake floated towards Millie's nostrils, dragging her back to the present.

'Okay, everyone, time for that part of the day I know you have all been waiting for.' Millie cast a smile in the direction of Carla, who was busy photographing everyone's masterpieces with her beloved Pentax camera. 'Let's taste our creations!'

She arranged the products of the group's labour on four huge china platters decorated with Claudia's signature logos. The first showcased a perfect selection of the patisserie she had made that morning, along with the miniature chocolate-orange roulades covered with chocolate ganache and the chilli-chocolate brownies baked by Ella. The second plate held the cakes made by Imogen and Julia, the third by Karen and Gracie, and the last one was piled high with the offerings belonging to Harriet and Carla.

'Well done, everyone. These all look absolutely amazing!' declared Ella, her mahogany eyes sparkling with pride.

'You're too kind,' laughed Harriet. 'My roulades look like a steamroller has reversed over them! I'm not sure I actually *want* to eat them.'

'You're right – we do initially taste with our eyes. But in my opinion, the most important part of any bake is its aroma and its taste. Don't forget – the Chocolate and Confetti course is not a competition. It's an opportunity for you to learn new skills and improve on old ones. By the end of the week – when we will be tackling chocolate eclairs and profiteroles – I promise you'll be making patisserie fit to grace any Parisian store.'

'I wouldn't bet on it,' murmured Carla, eyeing her caramelized madeleines with disdain.

'Okay. Let's dig in!'

'Mmm. Gracie, darling, your chilli-chocolate brownies are simply delicious,' said Karen, holding her hand under her chin to catch any crumbs, smiling widely at her daughter.

'Thanks, Mum. I think these biscuits are the best, though.'

Amid the cacophony of animated conversation, coupled with the soft strains of calypso music emanating from the radio in the corner and the ever-present backing track of the cicadas, everyone in the hen party indulged in their favourite pastime – eating chocolate in all its guises.

'Oh my God, Millie. These have got to be *the* most delicious chocolate tortes I've ever tasted!' declared Imogen, reaching for a second and trying to stuff it into her mouth whole.

'A little decorum, darling!'

'This is the best hen week ever,' continued Imogen, ignoring her mother's chastisement. 'Who else gets to indulge their love of all things cocoa-related *and* feast their eyes on that magnificent view at the same time?'

The women gravitated to the sun-bleached wraparound veranda overlooking the Soufrière bay. Millie took a moment to appreciate the most spectacular example of nature's artwork. To their left, the Gros Piton and Petit Piton mountains rose from the Caribbean Sea like the spikes of a slumbering dinosaur, their peaks melting into a soft eiderdown of cloud, their emerald interiors seemingly replete with legends, fairy tales and pirate stories. All this verdant beauty was set against the deep sapphire of the ocean, its surface dotted with tiny flecks of multi-coloured sails, cruise ships laden with tourists, and cargo ships trailing a ripple of cappuccino froth in their wake.

'It *is* beautiful, isn't it?'

'Stunning. I've had an amazing day, Millie. It's been something that everyone can get involved in. I know Mum has had a fantastic time, but so has Gracie. Thank you so much for everything.'

'You're welcome. I'm sorry Claudia wasn't able to be here.'

'Gosh, don't apologise. Okay, when Mum booked the course we were expecting the celebrated Claudia Croft to regale us with juicy anecdotes about her TV show and teach us a few of her personal techniques, but you and Ella have been fantastic. I can't believe you're a pastry chef at a tiny patisserie in Hammersmith. Why aren't you working in a prestigious restaurant in the West End, shouting about your Michelin star accolade from the rooftops?'

'Oh, well, you know, life gets in the way of our dreams sometimes. Maybe one day…'

Now was definitely not the time to divulge the details of her relationship catastrophe, especially not to Imogen, who was about to exchange her wedding vows in a no-expense-spared ceremony on the lawns of an elegant five-star hotel, courtesy of her architect fiancé, Alex Watson. But Imogen was right. She shouldn't be hiding in London whilst Luke continued to run the restaurant in Oxford where they had jointly achieved the coveted Michelin star.

However, the shock revelation of the identity of Luke's girlfriend had meant she'd had to get away. She hadn't been able to deal with the shame, and despite finding out that her best friend Frankie had been as much in the dark about Luke's betrayal as she had been, she had chosen to run away, to hotfoot it to London where she had landed her job at Étienne's Parisian Patisserie.

But now, after her extended stay in the Caribbean, she had mixed feelings about returning to her studio home amid the chimney pots and TV aerials. She loved the hustle and bustle of her new life in the capital, and the fantastic nights out with her fellow pastry chef and new best friend, Poppy. What she wasn't looking forward to were the dark, leaden skies, the terrible traffic fighting for supremacy on the city's streets, or the pressure from her family to fulfil her dream of one day running her own restaurant again after the heartache Luke's infidelity had caused.

A wave of tiredness rolled over her, her feet ached, but her overwhelming feeling was one of exhilaration. Now that the first day of the Paradise Cookery School had been a success, she couldn't wait to showcase what she and Ella had planned for the rest of the week. Maybe she *could* change her life by branching out into cookery demonstrations when she returned home? A splash of excitement burst into her chest at the prospect.

'I wish Alex and I were getting married here instead of up at the hotel,' mused Imogen, gazing down at the rectangle of aquamarine glittering in the sunshine on the terrace below the veranda, where Julia was stretched out on a sun lounger with a cocktail she had invented herself. 'It's exactly what Alex and I want. Small, intimate, friendly.'

'I think Claudia does have plans to offer guests of the Paradise Cookery School the chance to experience the full package; accommodation, gourmet meals and maybe even guided tours of the cocoa plantation. Since she bought the estate, it's always been her ambition to revitalise the crop and to produce her own Paradise cocoa beans one day. That's why they employed an estate manager last year to oversee the plantation.'

'You mean Zach? That handsome hunk who's taken the guys out on a rainforest scavenger hunt today?'

'Actually, no. I meant his colleague, Jake Lawson,' laughed Millie, her stomach performing a swift somersault at the mention of Zach's name. 'Zach manages Claudia's Cotswolds estate where she runs her UK cookery school. He did a swap so that Jake could go back home for a few months whilst his mother receives treatment for cancer.'

A sudden splat of rain landed on the wooden planks in front of Millie and Imogen, followed swiftly by several more.

'Oh, my God! Is it raining?'

'The locals call it liquid sunshine,' said Millie, smiling at the bride-to-be's wrinkled nose and upturned lip at the brief absence of the sun. 'Without the daily deluge, we wouldn't be feasting our eyes on all this tropical magnificence! Don't worry. It's just a shower, usual service will resume shortly.'

'This isn't a shower, it's a monsoon!' tutted Julia, dashing past them to shelter in the kitchen as the rain continued to hammer down with vicious acrimony. 'Would you like us to help you tidy up the kitchen?'

'No, thank you!' exclaimed Ella, in a tone that brooked no argument.

'It's very kind of you to offer, though,' said Millie, who privately would have loved to have taken Julia up on her offer. 'See you tomorrow – is a ten o'clock start okay?'

'Perfect.'